# VALTIERI'S BRIDE

BY

CAROLINE ANDERSON

All the characters in this book have no existence outside the imagination of the author, and have no relation whatsoever to anyone bearing the same name or names. They are not even distantly inspired by any individual known or unknown to the author, and all the incidents are pure invention.



First published in Great Britain 2012
by Mills & Boon, an imprint of Harlequin (UK) Limited.
Large Print edition 2012
Harlequin (UK) Limited, Eton House,
18-24 Paradise Road, Richmond, Surrey TW9 1SR



ISBN: 978 0 263 22610 2

Harlequin (UK) policy is to use papers that are natural, renewable and recyclable products and made from wood grown in sustainable forests. The logging and manufacturing process conform to the legal environmental regulations of the country of origin.

Printed and bound in Great Britain
by CPI Antony Rowe, Chippenham, Wiltshire

# CHAPTER ONE

WHAT *on earth* was she doing?

As the taxi pulled up in front of the Jet Centre at London City Airport, he paused, wallet in hand, and stared spellbound across the drop-off point.

Wow. She was *gorgeous.*

Even in the crazy fancy-dress outfit, her beauty shone out like a beacon. Her curves—soft, feminine curves—were in all the right places, and her face was alight with laughter, the skin pale and clear, her cheeks tinged pink by the long blonde curls whipping round her face in the cutting wind. She looked bright and alive and impossibly lovely, and he felt something squeeze in his chest.

Something that had been dormant for a very long time.

As he watched she anchored the curls absently with one hand, the other gesturing expressively as she smiled and talked to the man she'd stopped at the entrance. She was obviously selling something. Goodness knows what, he couldn't read the piece of card she was brandishing from this distance, but the man laughed and raised a hand in refusal and backed away, entering the building with a chuckle.

Her smile fading, she turned to her companion, more sensibly dressed in jeans and a little jacket. Massimo flicked his eyes over her, but she didn't hold his attention. Not like the blonde, and he found his eyes drawn back to her against his will.

*Dio*, she was exquisite. By rights she should have looked an utter tramp but somehow, even in the tacky low-cut dress and a gaudy plastic tiara, she was, quite simply, riveting. There was something about her that transcended all of that, and he felt himself inexplicably drawn to her.

He paid the taxi driver, hoisted his flight bag over his shoulder and headed for the entrance. She was busy again, talking to another man, and as the doors opened he caught her eye and she flashed a hopeful smile at him.

He didn't have time to pause, whatever she was selling, he thought regretfully, but the smile hit him in the solar plexus, and he set his bag down on the floor by the desk once he was inside, momentarily winded.

'Morning, Mr Valtieri. Welcome back to the Jet Centre. The rest of your party have arrived.'

'Thank you.' He cleared his throat and glanced over his shoulder at the woman. 'Is that some kind of publicity stunt?'

The official gave a quiet, mildly exasperated sigh and smiled wryly.

'No, sir. I understand she's trying to get a flight to Italy.'

Massimo felt his right eyebrow hike. 'In a *wedding dress*?'

He gave a slight chuckle. 'Apparently so. Some competition to win a wedding.'

He felt a curious sense of disappointment. Not that it made the slightest bit of difference that she was getting married; she was nothing to him and never would be, but nevertheless…

'We asked her to leave the building, but short of escorting her right back to the main road, there's little more we can do to get rid of her and she seems harmless enough. Our clients seem to be finding her quite entertaining, anyway.'

He could understand that. He was entertained

himself—mesmerised, if he was honest. And intrigued—

'Whereabouts in Italy?' he asked casually, although the tightness in his gut was far from casual.

'I think I heard her mention Siena—but, Mr Valtieri, you really don't want to get involved,' he warned, looking troubled. 'I think she's a little…'

'Crazy?' he said drily, and the man's mouth twitched.

'Your word, sir, not mine.'

As they watched, the other man walked away and she gave her companion a wry little smile. She said something, shrugged her slender shoulders in that ridiculous meringue of a dress, then rubbed her arms briskly. She must be freezing! September was a strange month, and today there wasn't a trace of sunshine and a biting wind was whipping up the Thames estuary.

No! It was none of his business if she hadn't had the sense to dress for the weather, he told himself firmly, but then he saw another man approach the doors, saw the woman straighten her spine and go up to him, her face wreathed in smiles as she launched into a fresh charm offensive, and he felt his gut clench.

He knew the man slightly, more by reputation than anything else, and he was absolutely the last person this enchanting and slightly eccentric young woman needed to get involved with. And he would be flying to his private airfield, about an hour's drive from Siena. Close enough, if you were desperate…

He couldn't let it happen. He had more than enough on his conscience.

The doors parted with a hiss as he strode up to them, and he gave the other man a look he had no trouble reading. He told him—in Italian, and succinctly—to back off, and Nico shrugged and took his advice, smiling regretfully at the woman before moving away from her, and Massimo gave him a curt nod and turned to the woman, meeting her eyes again—vivid, startling blue eyes that didn't look at all happy with what he'd just done. There was no smile this time, just those eyes like blue ice-chips skewering him as he stood there.

Stunning eyes, framed by long, dark lashes. Her mouth, even without the smile, was soft and full and kissable— No! He sucked in a breath, and found himself drawing a delicate and haunting fragrance into his lungs.

It rocked him for a second, took away his senses, and when they came back they *all* came back, slamming into him with the force of an express train and leaving him wanting in a way he hadn't wanted for years. Maybe ever—

'What did you *say* to him?' Lydia asked furiously, hardly able to believe the way he'd dismissed that man with a few choice words—not that she'd understood one of them, of course, but there was more to language than vocabulary and he'd been pretty explicit, she was sure. But she'd been so close to success and she was really, really cross and frustrated now. 'He'd just offered me a seat in his plane!'

'Believe me, you don't want to go on his plane.'

'Believe me, I do!' she retorted, but he shook his head.

'No. I'm sorry, I can't let you do it, it just isn't safe,' he said, a little crisply, and she dropped her head back and gave a sharp sigh.

Damn. He must be airport security, and a higher authority than the nice young man who'd shifted them outside. She sensed there'd be no arguing with him. There was a quiet implacability about him that reminded her of her father, and she knew when she was beaten. She met his eyes again, and tried not to notice that they were the colour of dark, bitter chocolate, warm and rich and really rather gorgeous.

And unyielding.

She gave up.

'I would have been perfectly safe, I've got a minder and I'm no threat to anyone and nobody's complained, as far as I know, but you can call the dogs off, I'm going.'

To her surprise he smiled, those amazing eyes softening and turning her bones to mush.

'Relax, I'm nothing to do with Security, I just have a social conscience. I believe you need to go to Siena?'

Siena? Nobody, she'd discovered, was flying to Siena but it seemed, incredibly, that he might be, or else why would he be asking? She stifled the little flicker of hope. 'I thought you said it wasn't safe?'

'It wasn't safe with *Nico*.'

'And it's safe with you?'

'Safer. My pilot won't have been drinking, and I—' He broke off, and watched her eyes widen as her mind filled in the blanks.

'And you?' she prompted a little warily, when he left it hanging there.

He sighed sharply and raked a hand through his hair, rumpling the dark strands threaded with silver at the temples. He seemed impatient, as if he was helping her against his better judgement. 'He has a—reputation,' he said finally.

She dragged her eyes off his hair. It had flopped forwards, and her fingers itched to smooth it back, to feel the texture…

'And you don't?'

'Let's just say that I respect women.' His mouth flickered in a wry smile. 'If you want a reference, my lawyer and doctor brothers would probably vouch for me, as would my three sisters—failing that, you could phone Carlotta. She's worked for the family for hundreds of years, and she delivered me and looks after my children.'

He had children? She glanced down and clocked the wedding ring on his finger, and with a sigh of relief, she thrust a laminated sheet at him and dug out her smile again. This time, it was far easier, and she felt a flicker of excitement burst into life.

'It's a competition to win a wedding at a hotel near Siena. There are two of us in the final leg, and I have to get to the hotel first to win the prize. This is Claire, she's from the radio station doing the publicity.'

Massimo gave Claire a cursory smile. He wasn't in the least interested in Claire. She was obviously the minder, and pretty enough, but this woman with the crazy outfit and sassy mouth…

He scanned the sheet, scanned it again, shook his head in disbelief and handed it back, frankly appalled. 'You must be mad. You have only a hundred pounds, a wedding dress and a passport, and you have to race to Siena to win this wedding? What on *earth* is your fiancé thinking of to let you do it?'

'Not my fiancé. I don't have a fiancé, and if I did, I wouldn't need his permission,' she said crisply, those eyes turning to ice again. 'It's for my sister. She had an accident, and they'd planned—oh, it doesn't matter. Either you can help me or you can't, and if you can't, the clock's ticking and I really have to get on.'

She didn't have a fiancé? 'I can help you,' he said before he could let himself think about it, and he thrust out his hand. 'Massimo Valtieri. If you're ready to go, I can give you a lift to Siena now.'

He pronounced it Mah-*see*-mo, long and slow and drawn out, his Italian accent coming over loud and clear as he said his name, and she felt a shiver of something primeval down her spine. Or maybe it was just the cold. She smiled at her self-appointed knight in shining armour and held out her hand.

'I'm Lydia Fletcher—and if you can get us there before the others, I'll love you forever.'

His warm, strong and surprisingly slightly calloused fingers closed firmly round hers, and she felt the world shift a little under her feet. And not just hers, apparently. She saw the shockwave hit his eyes, felt the recognition of something momentous passing between them, and in that crazy and insane instant she wondered if anything would ever be the same again.

The plane was small but, as the saying goes, perfectly formed.

Very perfectly, as far as she was concerned. It

had comfortable seats, lots of legroom, a sober pilot and a flight plan that without doubt would win her sister the wedding of her dreams.

Lydia could hardly believe her luck.

She buckled herself in, grabbed Claire's hand and hung on tight as the plane taxied to the end of the runway. 'We did it. We got a flight straight there!' she whispered, and Claire's face lit up with her smile, her eyes sparkling.

'I know. Amazing! We're going to do it. We can't fail. I just know you're going to win!'

The engines roared, the small plane shuddering, and then it was off like a slingshot, the force of their acceleration pushing her back hard into the leather seat as the jet tipped and climbed. The Thames was flying past, dropping rapidly below them as they rose into the air over London, and then they were heading out over the Thames estuary towards France, levelling off, and the seat belt light went out.

'Oh, this is so exciting! I'm going to update the diary,' Claire said, pulling out her little notebook computer, and Lydia turned her head and met Massimo's eyes across the narrow aisle.

He unclipped his seat belt and shifted his body

so he was facing her, his eyes scanning her face. His mouth tipped into a smile, and her stomach turned over—from the steep ascent, or from the warmth of that liquid-chocolate gaze?

'All right?'

'Amazing.' She smiled back, her mouth curving involuntarily in response to his, then turning down as she pulled a face. 'I don't know how to thank you. I'm so sorry I was rude.'

His mouth twitched. 'Don't worry. You weren't nearly as rude to me as I was to Nico.'

'What *did* you say to him?' she asked curiously, and he gave a soft laugh.

'I'm not sure it would translate. Certainly not in mixed company.'

'I think I got the gist—'

'I hope not!'

She gave a little laugh. 'Probably not. I don't know any street Italian—well, no Italian at all, really. And I feel awful now for biting your head off, but…well, it means a lot to me, to win this wedding.'

'Yes, I gather. You were telling me about your sister?' he said.

'Jennifer. She had an accident a few months

ago and she was in a wheelchair, but she's getting better, she's on crutches now, but her fiancé had to give up his job to help look after her. They're living with my parents and Andy's working with Dad at the moment for their keep. My parents have got a farm—well, not really a farm, more of a smallholding, really, but they get by, and they could always have the wedding there. There's a vegetable packing barn they could dress up for the wedding reception, but—well, my grandmother lived in Italy for a while and Jen's always dreamed of getting married there, and now they haven't got enough money even for a glass of cheap bubbly and a few sandwiches. So when I heard about this competition I just jumped at it, but I never in my wildest dreams imagined we'd get this far, never mind get a flight to exactly the right place. I'm just so grateful I don't know where to start.'

She was gabbling. She stopped, snapped her mouth shut and gave him a rueful grin. 'Sorry. I always talk a lot when the adrenaline's running.'

He smiled and leant back, utterly charmed by her. More than charmed…

'Relax. I have three sisters and two daughters, so I'm quite used to it, I've had a lot of practice.'

'Gosh, it sounds like it. And you've got two brothers as well?'

'*Si*. Luca's the doctor and he's married to an English girl called Isabelle, and Gio's the lawyer. I also have a son, and two parents, and a million aunts and uncles and cousins.'

'So what do you do?' she asked, irresistibly curious, and he gave her a slightly lopsided grin.

'You could say I'm a farmer, too. We grow grapes and olives and we make cheese.'

She glanced around at the plane. 'You must make a heck of a lot of cheese,' she said drily, and he chuckled, soft and low under his breath, just loud enough for her to hear.

The slight huff of his breath made an errant curl drift against her cheek, and it was almost as if his fingertips had brushed lightly against her skin.

'Not that much,' he said, his eyes still smiling. 'Mostly we concentrate on our wine and olive oil—Tuscan olive oil is sharper, tangier than the oil from southern Italy because we harvest the olives younger to avoid the frosts, and it gives it a distinctive and rich peppery flavour. But again, we don't make a huge amount, we concentrate on quality and aim for the boutique market with limited editions of certified, artisan products. That's what I was doing in England—I've been at a trade fair pushing our oil and wine to restaurateurs and gourmet delicatessens.'

She sat up straighter. 'Really? Did you take samples with you?'

He laughed. 'Of course. How else can I convince people that our products are the best? But the timing was bad, because we're about to harvest the grapes and I'm needed at home. That's why we chartered the plane, to save time.'

Chartered. So it wasn't his. That made him more approachable, somehow and, if it was possible, even more attractive. As did the fact that he was a farmer. She knew about farming, about aiming for a niche market and going for quality rather than quantity. It was how she'd been brought up. She relaxed, hitched one foot up under her and hugged her knee under the voluminous skirt.

'So, these samples—do you have any on the plane that I could try?'

'Sorry, we're out of wine,' he said, but then she laughed and shook her head.

'That's not what I meant, although I'm sure

it's very good. I was talking about the olive oil. Professional interest.'

'You grow olives on your farm in England?' he asked incredulously, and she laughed again, tightening his gut and sending need arrowing south. It shocked him slightly, and he forced himself to concentrate.

'No. Of course not. I've been living in a flat with a pot of basil on the window sill until recently! But I love food.'

'You mentioned a professional interest.'

She nodded. 'I'm a—' She was going to say chef, but could you be a chef if you didn't have a restaurant? If your kitchen had been taken away from you and you had nothing left of your promising career? 'I cook,' she said, and he got up and went to the rear of the plane and returned with a bottle of oil.

'Here.'

He opened it and held it out to her, and she sniffed it slowly, drawing the sharp, fruity scent down into her lungs. 'Oh, that's gorgeous. May I?'

And taking it from him, she tipped a tiny pool into her hand and dipped her finger into it, sucking the tip and making an appreciative noise. Heat slammed through him, and he recorked the bottle and put it away to give him something to do while he reassembled his brain.

He never, *never* reacted to a woman like this! What on earth was he thinking of? Apart from the obvious, but he didn't want to think about that. He hadn't looked at a woman in that way for years, hadn't thought about sex in he didn't know how long. So why now, why this woman?

She wiped up the last drop, sucking her finger again and then licking her palm, leaving a fine sheen of oil on her lips that he really, really badly want to kiss away.

'Oh, that is so good,' she said, rubbing her hands together to remove the last trace. 'It's a shame we don't have any bread or balsamic vinegar for dunking.'

He pulled a business card out of his top pocket and handed it to her, pulling his mind back into order and his eyes out of her cleavage. 'Email me your address when you get home, I'll send you some of our wine and oil, and also a traditional *aceto balsamico* made by my cousin in Modena. They only make a little, but it's the best I've ever tasted. We took some with us, but I haven't got any of that left, either.'

'Wow. Well, if it's as good as the olive oil, it must be fabulous!'

'It is. We're really proud of it in the family. It's nearly as good as our olive oil and wine.'

She laughed, as she was meant to, tucking the card into her bag, then she tipped her head on one side. 'Is it a family business?'

He nodded. 'Yes, most definitely. We've been there for more than three hundred years. We're very lucky. The soil is perfect, the slopes are all in the right direction, and if we can't grow one thing on any particular slope, we grow another, or use it for pasture. And then there are the chestnut woods. We export a lot of canned chestnuts, both whole and puréed.'

'And your wife?' she asked, her curiosity getting the better of her. 'Does she help with the business, or do you keep her too busy producing children for you?'

There was a heartbeat of silence before his eyes clouded, and his smile twisted a little as he looked away. 'Angelina died five years ago,' he said softly, and she felt a wave of regret that she'd blundered in and brought his grief to life when they'd been having a sensible and intelligent conversation about something she was genuinely interested in.

She reached across the aisle and touched his arm gently. 'I'm so sorry. I wouldn't have brought it up if…'

'Don't apologise. It's not your fault. Anyway, five years is a long time.'

Long enough that, when confronted by a vivacious, dynamic and delightful woman with beautiful, generous curves and a low-cut dress that gave him a more than adequate view of those curves, he'd almost forgotten his wife…

Guilt lanced through him, and he pulled out his wallet and showed her the photos—him and Angelina on their wedding day, and one with the girls clustered around her and the baby in her arms, all of them laughing. He loved that one. It was the last photograph he had of her, and one of the best. He carried it everywhere.

She looked at them, her lips slightly parted, and he could see the sheen of tears in her eyes.

'You must miss her so much. Your poor children.'

'It's not so bad now, but they missed her at first,'

he said gruffly. And he'd missed her. He'd missed her every single day, but missing her didn't bring her back, and he'd buried himself in work.

He was still burying himself in work.

Wasn't he?

Not effectively. Not any more, apparently, because suddenly he was beginning to think about things he hadn't thought about for years, and he wasn't ready for that. He couldn't deal with it, couldn't think about it. Not now. He had work to do, work that couldn't wait. Work he should be doing now.

He put the wallet away and excused himself, moving to sit with the others and discuss how to follow up the contacts they'd made and where they went from here with their marketing strategy, with his back firmly to Lydia and that ridiculous wedding dress that was threatening to tip him over the brink.

Lydia stared at his back, regret forming a lump in her throat.

She'd done it again. Opened her mouth and jumped in with both feet. She was good at that, gifted almost. And now he'd pulled away from her, and must be regretting the impulse that had made him offer her and Claire a lift to Italy.

She wanted to apologise, to take back her stupid and trite and intrusive question about his wife—Angelina, she thought, remembering the way he'd said her name, the way he'd almost tasted it as he said it, no doubt savouring the precious memories. But life didn't work like that.

Like feathers from a burst cushion, it simply wasn't possible to gather the words up and stuff them back in without trace. She just needed to move on from the embarrassing lapse, to keep out of his personal life and take his offer of a lift at face value.

And stop thinking about those incredible, warm chocolate eyes…

'I can't believe he's taking us right to Siena!' Claire said quietly, her eyes sparkling with delight. 'Jo will be so miffed when we get there first, she was so confident!'

Lydia dredged up her smile again, not hard when she thought about Jen and how deliriously happy she'd be to have her Tuscan wedding. 'I can't believe it, either. Amazing.'

Claire tilted her head on one side. 'What was he showing you? He looked sort of sad.'

She felt her smile slip. 'Photos of his wife. She died five years ago. They've got three little children—ten, seven and five, I think he said. Something like that.'

'Gosh. So the little one must have been tiny—did she die giving birth?'

'No. No, she can't have done. There was a photo of her with two little girls and a baby in her arms, so no. But it must have been soon after.'

'How awful. Fancy never knowing your mother. I'd die if I didn't have my mum to ring up and tell about stuff.'

Lydia nodded. She adored her mother, phoned her all the time, shared everything with her and Jen. What would it have been like never to have known her?

Tears welled in her eyes again, and she brushed them away crossly, but then she felt a light touch on her arm and looked up, and he was staring down at her, his face concerned.

He frowned and reached out a hand, touching the moisture on her cheek with a gentle fingertip.

'Lydia?'

She shook her head. 'I'm fine. Ignore me, I'm a sentimental idiot.'

He dropped to his haunches and took her hand, and she had a sudden and overwhelming urge to cry in earnest. 'I'm sorry. I didn't mean to distress you. You don't need to cry for us.'

She shook her head and sniffed again. 'I'm not. Not really. I was thinking about my mother—about how I'd miss her—and I'm twenty-eight, not five.'

He nodded. 'Yes. It's very hard.' His mouth quirked in a fleeting smile. 'I'm sorry, I've neglected you. Can I get you a drink? Tea? Coffee? Water? Something stronger?'

'It's a bit early for stronger,' she said, trying for a light note, and he smiled again, more warmly this time, and straightened up.

'Nico would have been on the second bottle of champagne by now,' he said, and she felt a wave of relief that he'd saved her from what sounded more and more like a dangerous mistake.

'Fizzy water would be nice, if you have any?' she said, and he nodded.

'Claire?'

'That would be lovely. Thank you.'

He moved away, and she let her breath out slowly. She hadn't really registered, until he'd crouched beside her, just how big he was. Not bulky, not in any way, but he'd shed his jacket and rolled up his shirtsleeves, and she'd been treated to the broad shoulders and solid chest at close range, and then his narrow hips and lean waist and those long, strong legs as he'd straightened up.

His hands, appearing in her line of sight again, were clamped round two tall glasses beaded with moisture and fizzing gently. Large hands, strong and capable, no-nonsense.

Safe, sure hands that had held hers and warmed her to the core.

Her breasts tingled unexpectedly, and she took the glass from him and tried not to drop it. 'Thank you.'

'*Prego*, you're welcome. Are you hungry? We have fruit and pastries, too.'

'No. No, I'm much too excited to eat now,' she confessed, sipping the water and hoping the cool liquid would slake the heat rising up inside her.

Crazy! He was totally uninterested in her, and even if he wasn't, she wasn't in the market for any more complications in her life. Her relationship with Russell had been fraught with complications, and the end of it had been a revelation. There was no way she was jumping back into that pond any time soon. The last frog she'd kissed had turned into a king-sized toad.

'How long before we land?' she asked, and he checked his watch, treating her to a bronzed, muscular forearm and strong-boned wrist lightly scattered with dark hair. She stared at it and swallowed. How ridiculous that an arm could be so sexy.

'Just over an hour. Excuse me, we have work to do, but please, if you need anything, just ask.'

He turned back to his colleagues, sitting down and flexing his broad shoulders, and Lydia felt her gut clench. She'd never, *never* felt like that about anyone before, and she couldn't believe she was reacting to him that way. It must just be the adrenaline.

One more hour to get through before they were there and they could thank him and get away—hopefully before she disgraced herself. The poor man was still grieving for his wife. What was she thinking about?

Ridiculous! She'd known him, what, less than

two hours altogether? Scarcely more than one. And she'd already put her foot firmly in it.

Vowing not to say another thing, she settled back in her seat and looked out of the window at the mountains.

They must be the Alps, she realised, fascinated by the jagged peaks and plunging valleys, and then the mountains fell away behind them and they were moving over a chequered landscape of forests and small, neat fields. They were curiously ordered and disciplined, serried ranks of what must be olive trees and grape vines, she guessed, planted with geometric precision, the pattern of the fields interlaced with narrow winding roads lined with avenues of tall, slender cypress trees.

Tuscany, she thought with a shiver of excitement.

The seat belt light came on, and Massimo returned to his seat across the aisle from her as the plane started its descent.

'Not long now,' he said, flashing her a smile. And then they were there, a perfect touchdown on Tuscan soil with the prize almost in reach.

Jen was going to get her wedding. Just a few more minutes…

They taxied to a stop outside the airport building, and after a moment the steps were wheeled out to them and the door was opened.

'We're really here!' she said to Claire, and Claire's eyes were sparkling as she got to her feet.

'I know. I can't believe it!'

They were standing at the top of the steps now, and Massimo smiled and gestured to them. 'After you. Do you have the address of the hotel? I'll drive you there.'

'Are you sure?'

'I'd hate you not to win after all this,' he said with a grin.

'Wow, thank you, that's really kind of you!' Lydia said, reaching for her skirts as she took another step.

It happened in slow motion.

One moment she was there beside him, the next the steps had disappeared from under her feet and she was falling, tumbling end over end, hitting what seemed like every step until finally her head reached the tarmac and she crumpled on the ground in a heap.

Her scream was cut off abruptly, and Massimo hurled himself down the steps to her side, his heart racing. No! Please, she couldn't be dead…

She wasn't. He could feel a pulse in her neck, and he let his breath out on a long, ragged sigh and sat back on his heels to assess her.

Stay calm, he told himself. She's alive. She'll be all right.

But he wouldn't really believe it until she stirred, and even then…

'Is she all right?'

He glanced up at Claire, kneeling on the other side of her, her face chalk white with fear.

'I think so,' he said, but he didn't think any such thing. Fear was coursing through him, bringing bile rising to his throat. Why wasn't she moving? This couldn't be happening again.

Lydia moaned. Warm, hard fingers had searched for a pulse in her neck, and as she slowly came to, she heard him snap out something in Italian while she lay there, shocked and a little stunned, wondering if it was a good idea to open her eyes. Maybe not yet.

'Lydia? Lydia, talk to me! Open your eyes.'

Her eyes opened slowly and she tried to sit up, but he pressed a hand to her shoulder.

'Stay still. You might have a neck injury. Where do you hurt?'

Where didn't she? She turned her head and winced. 'Ow…my head, for a start. What happened? Did I trip? Oh, I can't believe I was so stupid!'

'You fell down the steps.'

'I know that—ouch.' She felt her head, and her hand came away bloodied and sticky. She stared at it. 'I've cut myself,' she said, and everything began to swim.

'It's OK, Lydia. You'll be OK,' Claire said, but her face was worried and suddenly everything began to hurt a whole lot more.

Massimo tucked his jacket gently beside her head to support it, just in case she had a neck injury. He wasn't taking any chances on that, but it was the head injury that was worrying him the most, the graze on her forehead, just under her hair. How hard had she hit it? Hard enough to…

It was bleeding faster now, he realised with a wave of dread, a red streak appearing as she shifted slightly, and he stayed beside her on his knees, holding her hand and talking to her comfortingly in between snapping out instructions.

She heard the words '*ambulanza*' and '*ospedale*', and tried to move, wincing and whimpering with pain, but he held her still.

'Don't move. The ambulance is coming to take you to hospital.'

'I don't need to go to hospital, I'm fine, we need to get to the hotel!'

'No,' Massimo and Claire said in unison.

'But the competition.'

'It doesn't matter,' he said flatly. 'You're hurt. You have to be checked out.'

'I'll go later.'

'No.' His voice was implacable, hard and cold and somehow strange, and Lydia looked at him and saw his skin was colourless and grey, his mouth pinched, his eyes veiled.

He obviously couldn't stand the sight of blood, Lydia realised, and reached out her other hand to Claire.

She took it, then looked at Massimo. 'I'll look after her,' she said. 'You go, you've got lots to do. We'll be all right.'

His eyes never left Lydia's.

'No. I'll stay with you,' he insisted, but he moved out of the way to give her space.

She looked so frail suddenly, lying there streaked with blood, the puffy layers of the dress rising up around her legs and making her look like a broken china doll.

*Dio*, he felt sick just looking at her, and her face swam, another face drifting over it. He shut his eyes tight, squeezing out the images of his wife, but they refused to fade.

Lydia tried to struggle up again. 'I want to go to the hotel,' she said to Claire, and his eyes snapped open again.

'No way.'

'He's right. Don't be silly. You just lie there and we'll get you checked out, then we'll go. There's still plenty of time.'

But there might not be, she realised, as she lay there on the tarmac in her ridiculous charity shop wedding dress with blood seeping from her head wound, and as the minutes ticked by her joy slid slowly away…

# CHAPTER TWO

THE ambulance came, and Claire went with Lydia.

He wanted to go with her himself, he felt he ought to, felt the weight of guilt and worry like an elephant on his chest, but it wasn't his place to accompany her, so Claire went, and he followed in his car, having sent the rest of the team on with a message to his family that he'd been held up but would be with them as soon as he could.

He rang Luca on the way, in case he was there at the hospital in Siena that day as he sometimes was, and his phone was answered instantly.

'Massimo, welcome home. Good flight?'

He nearly laughed. 'No. Where are you? Which hospital?'

'Siena. Why?'

He did laugh then. Or was it a sob of relief? 'I'm on my way there. I gave two girls a lift in the plane, and one of them fell down the steps as we were disembarking. I'm following the ambulance. Luca, she's got a head injury,' he added, his heart pounding with dread, and he heard his brother suck in his breath.

'I'll meet you in the emergency department. She'll be all right, Massimo. We'll take care of her.'

He grunted agreement, switched off the phone and followed the ambulance, focusing on facts and crushing his fear and guilt down. It couldn't happen again. Lightning didn't strike twice, he told himself, and forced himself to follow the ambulance at a sensible distance while trying desperately to put Angelina firmly out of his mind…

Luca was waiting for him at the entrance.

He took the car away to park it and Massimo hovered by the ambulance as they unloaded Lydia and whisked her inside, Claire holding her hand and reassuring her. It didn't sound as if it was working, because she kept fretting about the competition and insisting she was all right when anyone could see she was far from all right.

She was taken away, Claire with her, and he stayed in the waiting area, pacing restlessly and driving himself mad with his imagination of what was happening beyond the doors. His brother reappeared moments later and handed him the keys, giving him a keen look.

'You all right?'

Hardly. 'I'm fine,' he said, his voice tight.

'So how do you know this woman?' Luca asked, and he filled him in quickly with the bare bones of the accident.

'Oh—she's wearing a wedding dress,' he warned. 'It's a competition, a race to win a wedding.'

A race she'd lost. If only he'd taken her arm, or gone in front, she would have fallen against him, he could have saved her…

'Luca, don't let her die,' he said urgently, fear clawing at him.

'She won't die,' Luca promised, although how he could say that without knowing—well, he couldn't. It was just a platitude, Massimo knew that.

'Let me know how she is.'

Luca nodded and went off to investigate, leaving him there to wait, but he felt bile rise in his throat and got abruptly to his feet, pacing restlessly again. How long could it take?

Hours, apparently, or at least it felt like it.

Luca reappeared with Claire.

'They're taking X-rays of her leg now but it looks like a sprained ankle. She's just a little concussed and bruised from her fall, but the head injury doesn't look serious,' he said.

'Nor did Angelina's,' he said, switching to Italian.

'She's not Angelina, Massimo. She's not going to die of this.'

'Are you sure?'

'Yes. Yes, I'm sure. She's had a scan. She's fine.'

It should have reassured him, but Massimo felt his heart still slamming against his ribs, the memories crowding him again.

'She's all right,' Luca said quietly. 'This isn't the same.'

He nodded, but he just wanted to get out, to be away from the hospital in the fresh air. Not going to happen. He couldn't leave Lydia, no matter how much he wanted to get away. And he could never get away from Angelina…

Luca took him to her.

She was lying on a trolley, and there was blood streaked all over the front of the hideous dress, but at least they'd taken her off the spinal board. 'How are you?' he asked, knowing the answer but having to ask anyway, and she turned her head and met his eyes, her own clouded with worry and pain.

'I'm fine, they just want to watch me for a while. I've got some bumps and bruises, but nothing's broken, I'm just sore and cross with myself and I want to go to the hotel and they won't let me leave yet. I'm so sorry, Massimo, I've got Claire, you don't need to wait here with me. It could be ages.'

'I do.' He didn't explain, didn't tell her what she didn't need to know, what could only worry her. But he hadn't taken Angelina's head injury seriously. He'd assumed it was nothing. He hadn't watched her, sat with her, checked her every few minutes. If he had—well, he hadn't, but he was damned if he was leaving Lydia alone for a moment until he was sure she was all right.

Luca went back to work, and while the doctors checked her over again and strapped her ankle, Massimo found some coffee for him and Claire and they sat and drank it. Not a good idea. The caffeine shot was the last thing his racing pulse needed.

'I need to make a call,' Claire told him. 'If I go just outside, can you come and get me if there's any news?'

He nodded, watching her leave. She was probably phoning the radio station to tell them about Lydia's accident. And she'd been so close to winning…

She came back, a wan smile on her face. 'Jo's there.'

'Jo?'

'The other contestant. Lydia's lost the race. She's going to be so upset. I can't tell her yet.'

'I think you should. She might stop fretting if it's too late, let herself relax and get better.'

Claire gave a tiny, slightly hysterical laugh. 'You don't know her very well, do you?'

He smiled ruefully. 'No. No, I don't.' And it was ridiculous that he minded the fact.

Lydia looked up as they went back in, and she scanned Claire's face.

'Did you ring the radio station?'

'Yes.'

'Has…' She could hardly bring herself to ask the question, but she took another breath and tried again. 'Has Jo got there yet?' she asked, and then held her breath. It was possible she'd been unlucky, that she hadn't managed to get a flight, that any one of a hundred things could have happened.

They hadn't. She could see it in Claire's eyes, she didn't need to be told that Jo and Kate, her minder, were already there, and she felt the bitter sting of tears scald her eyes.

'She's there, isn't she?' she asked, just because she needed confirmation.

Claire nodded, and Lydia turned her head away, shutting her eyes against the tears. She was so, *so* cross with herself. They'd been so close to winning, and if she'd only been more careful, gathered up the stupid dress so she could see the steps.

She swallowed hard and looked back up at Claire's worried face. 'Tell her well done for me when you see her.'

'I will, but you'll see her, too. We've got rooms in the hotel for the night. I'll ring them now, let them know what's happening. We can go there when they discharge you.'

'No, I could be ages. Why don't you go, have a

shower and something to eat, see the others and I'll get them to ring you if there's any change. Or better still, if you give me back my phone and my purse, I can call you and let you know when I'm leaving, and I'll just get a taxi.'

'I can't leave you alone!'

'She won't be alone, I'll stay with her. I'm staying anyway, whether you're here or not,' Massimo said firmly, and Lydia felt a curious sense of relief. Relief, and guilt.

And she could see the same emotions in Claire's face. She was dithering, chewing her lip in hesitation, and Lydia took her hand and squeezed it.

'There, you see? And his brother works here, so he'll be able to pull strings. It's fine, Claire. Just go. I'll see you later.' And she could get rid of Massimo once Claire had gone…

Claire gave in, reluctantly. 'OK, if you insist. Here, your things. I'll put them in your bag. Where is it?'

'I have no idea. Is it under the bed?'

'No. I haven't seen it.'

'It must have been left on the ground at the airport,' Massimo said. 'My men will have picked it up.'

'Can you check? My passport's in it.'

*'Si.'* He left them briefly, and when he came back he confirmed it had been taken by the others. 'I'll make sure you get it tonight,' he promised.

'Thanks. Right, Claire, you go. I'm fine.'

'You will call me and let me know what's going on as soon as you have any news?'

'Yes, I promise.'

Claire gave in, hugging Lydia a little tearfully before she left them.

Lydia swallowed. Damn. She was going to join in.

'Hey, it's all right. You'll be OK.'

His voice was gentle, reassuring, and his touch on her cheek was oddly comforting. Her eyes filled again.

'I'm causing everyone so much trouble.'

'That's life. Don't worry about it. Are you going to tell your family?'

Oh, cripes. She ought to phone Jen, but she couldn't. Not now. She didn't think she could talk to her just yet.

'Maybe later. I just feel so sleepy.'

'So rest. I'll sit with you.'

Sit with her and watch her. Do what he should have done years ago.

She shut her eyes, just for a moment, but when she opened them again he'd moved from her side. She felt a moment of panic, but then she saw him. He was standing a few feet away reading a poster about head injuries, his hands rammed in his pockets, tension radiating off him.

Funny, she'd thought it was because of the blood, but there was no sign of blood now apart from a dried streak on her dress. Maybe it was hospitals generally. Had Angelina been ill for a long time?

Or maybe hospitals just brought him out in hives. She could understand that. After Jen's accident, she felt the same herself, and yet he was still here, still apparently labouring under some misguided sense of obligation.

He turned his head, saw she was awake and came back to her side, his dark eyes searching hers.

'Are you all right?'

She nodded. 'My head's feeling clearer now. I need to ring Jen,' she said quietly, and he sighed and cupped her cheek, his thumb smoothing away a tear she hadn't realised she'd shed.

'I'm sorry, *cara*. I know how much it meant to you to win this for your sister.'

'It doesn't matter,' she said dismissively, although of course it would to Jen. 'It was just a crazy idea. They can get married at home, it's really not an issue. I really didn't think I'd win anyway, so we haven't lost anything.'

'Claire said Jo's been there for ages. She would probably have beaten you to it anyway,' he said. 'She must have got away very fast.'

She didn't believe it. He was only trying to make it better, to take the sting out of it, but before she had time to argue the doctor came back in, checked her over and delivered her verdict.

Massimo translated.

'You're fine, you need to rest for a few days before you fly home, and you need watching overnight, but you're free to go.'

She thanked the doctor, struggled up and swung her legs over the edge of the trolley, and paused for a moment, her head swimming.

'All right?'

'I'm fine. I need to call a taxi to take me to the hotel.'

'I'll give you a lift.'

'I can't take you out of your way! I've put you to enough trouble as it is. I can get a taxi. I'll be fine.'

But as she slid off the edge of the trolley and straightened up, Massimo caught the sheen of tears in her eyes.

Whatever she'd said, the loss of this prize was tearing her apart for her sister, and he felt guilt wash over him yet again. Logically, he knew he had no obligation to her, no duty that extended any further than simply flying her to Siena as he'd promised. But somehow, somewhere along the way, things had changed and he could no more have left her there at the door of the hospital than he could have left one of his children. And they were waiting for him, had been waiting for him far too long, and guilt tugged at him again.

'Ouch!'

'You can't walk on that ankle. Stay here.'

She stayed, wishing her flight bag was still with her instead of having been whisked away by his team. She could have done with changing out of the dress, but her comfy jeans and soft cotton top were in her bag, and she wanted to cry with frustration and disappointment and pain.

'Here.'

He'd brought a wheelchair, and she eyed it doubtfully.

'I don't know if the dress will fit in it. Horrible thing! I'm going to burn it just as soon as I get it off.'

'Good idea,' he said drily, and they exchanged a smile.

He squashed it in around her, and wheeled her towards the exit. Then he stopped the chair by the door and looked down at her.

'Do you really want to go to the hotel?' he asked.

She tipped her head back to look at him, but it hurt, and she let her breath out in a gusty sigh. 'I don't have a choice. I need a bed for the night, and I can't afford anywhere else.'

He moved so she could see him, crouching down beside her. 'You do have a choice. You can't fly for a few days, and you don't want to stay in a strange hotel on your own for all that time. And anyway, you don't have your bag, so why don't you come back with me?' he said, the guilt about his children growing now and the solution to both problems suddenly blindingly obvious.

'I need to get home to see my children, they've

been patient long enough, and you can clean up there and change into your own comfortable clothes and have something to eat and a good night's sleep. Carlotta will look after you.'

Carlotta? Lydia scanned their earlier conversations and came up with the name. She was the woman who looked after his children, who'd worked for them for a hundred years, as he'd put it, and had delivered him.

Carlotta sounded good.

'That's such an imposition. Are you sure you don't mind?'

'I'm sure. It's by far the easiest thing for me. The hotel's the other way, and it would save me a lot of time I don't really have, especially by the time I've dropped your bag over there. And you don't honestly want to be there on your own for days, do you?'

Guilt swamped her, heaped on the disappointment and the worry about Jen, and she felt crushed under the weight of it all. She felt her spine sag, and shook her head. 'I'm so sorry. I've wasted your entire day. If you hadn't given me a lift…'

'Don't go there. What ifs are a waste of time. Yes or no?'

'Yes, please,' she said fervently. 'That would be really kind.'

'Don't mention it. I feel it's all my fault anyway.'

'Rubbish. Of course it's not your fault. You've done so much already, and I don't think I've even thanked you.'

'You have. You were doing that when you fell down the steps.'

'Was I?' She gave him a wry grin, and turned to look up at him as they arrived at the car, resting her hand on his arm lightly to reassure him. 'It's really not your fault, you know.'

'I know. You missed your step. I know this. I still…'

He was still haunted, because of the head injury, images of Angelina crowding in on him. Angelina falling, Angelina with a headache, Angelina slumped over the kitchen table with one side of her face collapsed. Angelina linked up to a life support machine…

'Massimo?'

'I'm all right,' he said gruffly, and pressing the remote, he opened the door for her and settled her in, then returned the wheelchair and slid into the driver's seat beside her. 'Are you OK?'

'I'm fine.'

'Good. Let's go.'

She phoned Claire and told her what was happening, assured her she would be all right and promised to phone her the next day, then put the phone down in her lap and rested her head back.

Under normal circumstances, she thought numbly, she'd be wallowing in the luxury of his butter-soft leather, beautifully supportive car seats, or taking in the picture-postcard countryside of Tuscany as the car wove and swooped along the narrow winding roads.

As it was she gazed blankly at it all, knowing that she'd have to phone Jen, knowing she should have done it sooner, that her sister would be on tenterhooks, but she didn't have the strength to crush her hopes and dreams.

'Have you told your sister yet?' he asked, as if he'd read her mind.

She shook her head. 'No. I don't know what to say. If I hadn't fallen, we would have won. Easily. It was just so stupid, so clumsy.'

He sighed, his hand reaching out and closing over hers briefly, the warmth of it oddly comforting in a disturbing way. 'I'm sorry. Not because I feel it was my fault, because I know it wasn't, really, but because I know how it feels to let someone down, to have everyone's hopes and dreams resting on your shoulders, to have to carry the responsibility for someone else's happiness.'

She turned towards him, inhibited by the awful, scratchy dress that she couldn't wait to get out of, and studied his profile.

Strong. Clean cut, although no longer clean-shaven, the dark stubble that shadowed his jaw making her hand itch to feel the texture of it against her palm. In the dusk of early evening his olive skin was darker, somehow exotic, and with a little shiver she realised she didn't know him at all. He could be taking her anywhere.

She closed her eyes and told herself not to be ridiculous. He'd followed them to the hospital, got his brother in on the act, a brother she'd heard referred to as *il professore*, and now he was taking her to his family home, to his children, his parents, the woman who'd delivered him all those years ago. Forty years? Maybe. Maybe more, maybe less, but give or take.

Someone who'd stayed with the family for all

that time, who surely wouldn't still be there if they were nasty people?

'What's wrong?'

She shrugged, too honest to lie. 'I was just thinking, I don't know you. You could be anyone. After all, I was going in the plane with Nico, and you've pointed out in no uncertain terms that that wouldn't have been a good idea, and I just don't think I'm a very good judge of character.'

'Are you saying you don't trust me?'

She found herself smiling. 'Curiously, I do, or I wouldn't be here with you.'

He flashed her a look, and his mouth tipped into a wry grin. 'Well, thanks.'

'Sorry. It wasn't meant to sound patronising. It's just been a bit of a whirlwind today, and I'm not really firing on all cylinders.'

'I'm sure you're not. Don't worry, you're safe with me, I promise, and we're nearly there. You can have a long lazy shower, or lie in the bath, or have a swim. Whatever you choose.'

'So long as I can get out of this horrible dress, I'll be happy.'

He laughed, the sound filling the car and making something deep inside her shift.

'Good. Stand by to be happy very soon.'

He turned off the road onto a curving gravelled track lined by cypress trees, winding away towards what looked like a huge stone fortress. She sat up straighter. 'What's that building?'

'The house.'

'House?' She felt her jaw drop, and shut her mouth quickly. That was their *house*?

'So…is this your land?'

*'Si.'*

She stared around her, but the light was fading and it was hard to tell what she was looking at. But the massive edifice ahead of them was outlined against the sunset, and as they drew closer she could see lights twinkling in the windows.

They climbed the hill, driving through a massive archway and pulling up in front of a set of sweeping steps. Security lights came on as they stopped, and she could see the steps were flanked by huge terracotta pots with what looked like olive trees in them. The steps rose majestically up to the biggest set of double doors she'd ever seen in her life. Strong doors, doors that would keep you safe against all invaders.

She had to catch her jaw again, and for once

in her life she was lost for words. She'd thought, foolishly, it seemed, that it might shrink as they got closer, but it hadn't. If anything it had grown, and she realised it truly was a fortress.

An ancient, impressive and no doubt historically significant fortress. And it was his family home?

She thought of their modest farmhouse, the place she called home, and felt the sudden almost overwhelming urge to laugh. What on earth did he think of her, all tarted up in her ludicrous charity shop wedding dress and capering about outside the airport begging a lift from any old stranger?

'Lydia?'

He was standing by her, the door open, and she gathered up the dress and her purse and phone and squirmed off the seat and out of the car, balancing on her good leg and eyeing the steps dubiously.

How on earth—?

No problem, apparently. He shut the car door, and then to her surprise he scooped her up into his arms.

She gave a little shriek and wrapped her arms around his neck, so that her nose was pressed close to his throat in the open neck of his shirt. Oh, God. He smelt of lemons and musk and warm, virile male, and she could feel the beat of his heart against her side.

Or was it her own? She didn't know. It could have been either.

He glanced down at her, concerned that he might be hurting her. There was a little frown creasing the soft skin between her brows, and he had the crazy urge to kiss it away. He almost did, but stopped himself in time.

She was a stranger, nothing more, and he tried to ignore the feel of her against his chest, the fullness of her breasts pressing into his ribs and making his heart pound like a drum. She had her head tucked close to his shoulder, and he could feel the whisper of her breath against his skin. Under the antiseptic her hair smelled of fresh fruit and summer flowers, and he wanted to bury his face in it and breathe in.

He daren't look down again, though. She'd wrapped her arms around his neck and the front of the dress was gaping slightly, the soft swell of those beautiful breasts tempting him almost beyond endurance.

Crazy. Stupid. Whatever was the matter with

him? He gritted his teeth, shifted her a little closer and turned towards the steps.

Lydia felt his body tense, saw his jaw tighten and she wondered why. She didn't have time to work it out, though, even if she could, because as he headed towards the house three children came tumbling down the steps and came to a sliding halt in front of them, their mouths open, their faces shocked.

*'Pàpa?'*

The eldest, a thin, gangly girl with a riot of dark curls and her father's beautiful eyes, stared from one of them to the other, and the look on her face was pure horror.

'I think you'd better explain to your children that I am *not* your new wife,' she said drily, and the girl glanced back at her and then up at her father again.

*'Pàpa?'*

He was miles away, caught up in a fairy-tale fantasy of carrying this beautiful woman over the threshold and then peeling away the layers of her bridal gown…

'Massimo? I think you need to explain to the children,' Lydia said softly, watching his face at close range. There was a tic in his jaw, the muscle jumping. Had he carried Angelina up these steps?

'It's all right, Francesca,' he said in English, struggling to find his voice. 'This is Miss Fletcher. I met her today at the airport, and she's had an accident and has to rest for a few days, so I've brought her here. Say hello.'

She frowned and asked something in Italian, and he smiled a little grimly and shook his head. 'No. We are *not* married. Say hello to Miss Fletcher, *cara*.'

'Hello, Miss Fletcher,' Francesca said in careful English, her smile wary but her shoulders relaxing a little, and Lydia smiled back at her. She felt a little awkward, gathered up in his arms against that hard, broad chest with the scent of his body doing extraordinary things to her heart, but there was nothing she could do about it except smile and hope his arms didn't break.

'Hello, Francesca. Thank you for speaking English so I can understand you.'

'That's OK. We have to speak English to Auntie Isabelle. This is Lavinia, and this is Antonino. Say hello,' she prompted.

Lydia looked at the other two, clustered round

their sister. Lavinia was the next in line, with the same dark, glorious curls but mischief dancing in her eyes, and Antonino, leaning against Francesca and squiggling the toe of his shoe on the gravel, was the youngest. The baby in the photo, the little one who must have lost his mother before he ever really knew her.

Her heart ached for them all, and she felt a welling in her chest and crushed it as she smiled at them.

'Hello, Lavinia, hello, Antonino. It's nice to meet you,' she said, and they replied politely, Lavinia openly studying her, her eyes brimming over with questions.

'And this is Carlotta,' Massimo said, and she lifted her head and met searching, wise eyes in a wizened face. He spoke rapidly to her in Italian, explaining her ridiculous fancy-dress outfit no doubt, and she saw the moment he told her that they'd lost the competition, because Carlotta's face softened and she looked at Lydia and shook her head.

'Sorry,' she said, lifting her hands. 'So sorry for you. Come, I help you change and you will be happier, *si*?'

*'Si,'* she said with a wry chuckle, and Massimo shifted her more firmly against his chest and followed Carlotta puffing and wheezing up the steps.

The children were tugging at him and questioning him in Italian, and he was laughing and answering them as fast as he could. Bless their little hearts, she could see they were hanging on his every word.

He was the centre of their world, and they'd missed him, and she'd kept him away from them all these hours when they must have been desperate to have him back. She felt another shaft of guilt, but Carlotta was leading the way through the big double doors, and she looked away from the children and gasped softly.

They were in a cloistered courtyard, with a broad covered walkway surrounding the open central area that must cast a welcome shade in the heat of the day, but now in the evening it was softly lit and she could see more of the huge pots of olive trees set on the old stone paving in the centre, and on the low wall that divided the courtyard from the cloistered walkway geraniums tumbled over the edge, bringing colour and scent to the evening air.

But that wasn't what had caught her attention. It was the frescoed walls, the ancient faded murals under the shelter of the cloisters that took her breath away.

He didn't pause, though, or give her time to take in the beautiful paintings, but carried her through one of the several doors set in the walls, then along a short hallway and into a bedroom.

He set her gently on the bed, and she felt oddly bereft as he straightened up and moved away.

'I'll be in the kitchen with the children. Carlotta will tell me when you're ready and I'll come and get you.'

'Thank you.'

He smiled fleetingly and went out, the children's clamouring voices receding as he walked away, and Carlotta closed the door.

'Your bath,' she said, pushing open another door, and she saw a room lined with pale travertine marble, the white suite simple and yet luxurious. And the bath—she could stick her bandaged leg up on the side and just wallow. Pure luxury.

'Thank you.' She couldn't wait. All she wanted was to get out of the dress and into water. But the zip…

'I help you,' Carlotta said, and as the zip slid down, she was freed from the scratchy fabric at last. A bit too freed. She clutched at the top as it threatened to drift away and smiled at Carlotta.

'I can manage now,' she said, and Carlotta nodded.

'I get your bag.'

She went out, and Lydia closed the bedroom door behind her, leaning back against it and looking around again.

It was much simpler than the imposing and impressive entrance, she saw with relief. Against expectations it wasn't vast, but it was pristine, the bed made up with sparkling white linen, the rug on the floor soft underfoot, and the view from the French window would be amazing in daylight.

She limped gingerly over to the window and stared out, pressing her face against the glass. The doors opened onto what looked like a terrace, and beyond—gosh, the view must be utterly breathtaking, she imagined, because even at dusk it was extraordinary, the twinkling lights of villages and scattered houses sparkling in the twilight.

Moving away from the window, she glanced around her, taking in her surroundings in more detail. The floor was tiled, the ceiling beamed, with chestnut perhaps? Probably, with terracotta tiles between the beams. Sturdy, simple and homely—which was crazy, considering the scale of the place and the grandeur of the entrance! But it seemed more like a farm now, curiously, less of a fortress, and much less threatening.

And that established, she let go of the awful dress, kicked it away from her legs, bundled it up in a ball and hopped into the bathroom.

The water was calling her. Studying the architecture could wait.

# CHAPTER THREE

*WHAT was that noise?*

Lydia lifted her head, water streaming off her hair as she surfaced to investigate.

*'Signorina? Signorina!'*

Carlotta's voice was desperate as she rattled the handle on the bathroom door, and Lydia felt a stab of alarm.

'What is it?' she asked, sitting up with a splash and sluicing the water from her hair with her hands.

'Oh, *signorina*! You are all right?'

She closed her eyes and twisted her hair into a rope, squeezing out the rest of the water and suppressing a sigh. 'I'm fine. I'm OK, really. I won't be long.'

'I wait, I help you.'

'No, really, there's no need. I'll be all right.'

'But Massimo say I no leave you!' she protested,

clearly worried for some reason, but Lydia assured her again that she was fine.

'OK,' she said after a moment, sounding dubious. 'I leave your bag here. You call me for help?'

'I will. Thank you. *Grazie.*'

*'Prego.'*

She heard the bedroom door close, and rested her head back down on the bath with a sigh. The woman was kindness itself, but Lydia just wanted to be left alone. Her head ached, her ankle throbbed, she had a million bruises all over her body and she still had to phone her sister.

The phone rang, almost as if she'd triggered it with her thoughts, and she could tell by the ringtone it was Jen.

Oh, rats. She must have heard the news.

There was no getting round it, so she struggled awkwardly out of the bath and hobbled back to the bed, swathed in the biggest towel she'd ever seen, and dug out her phone and rang Jen back.

'What's going on? They said you'd had an accident! I've been trying to phone you for ages but you haven't been answering! Are you all right? We've been frantic!'

'Sorry, Jen, I was in the bath. I'm fine, really,

it was just a little slip on the steps of a plane and I've twisted my ankle. Nothing serious.'

Well, she hoped it wasn't. She crossed her fingers, just to be on the safe side, and filled in a few more details. She didn't tell her the truth, just that Jo had got there first.

'I'm so sorry, we really tried, but we probably wouldn't have made it even without the accident.'

There was a heartbeat of hesitation, then Jen said, 'Don't worry, it really doesn't matter and it's not important. I just need you to be all right. And don't go blaming yourself, it's not your fault.'

Why did *everyone* say that? It *was* her fault. If she'd looked where she was going, taken a bit more care, Jen and Andy would have been having the wedding of their dreams in a few months' time. As it was, well, as it was they wouldn't, but she wasn't going to give Jen anything to beat herself up about, so she told her she was fine, just a little twinge—and nothing at all about the head injury.

'Actually, since I'm over here, I thought I'd stay on for a few days. I've found a farm where I can get bed and breakfast, and I'm going to have a little holiday.'

Well, it wasn't entirely a lie. It *was* a farm, she had a bed, and she was sure they wouldn't make her starve while she recovered.

'You do that. It sounds lovely,' Jen said wistfully, and Lydia screwed her face up and bit her lip.

Damn. She'd been so close, and the disappointment that Jen was trying so hard to disguise was ripping Lydia apart.

Ending the call with a promise to ring when she was coming home, she dug her clean clothes out of the flight bag and pulled her jeans on carefully over her swollen, throbbing ankle. The soft, worn fabric of the jeans and the T-shirt were comforting against her skin, chafed from her fall as well as the boning and beading in the dress, and she looked around for the offending article. It was gone. Taken away by Carlotta? She hoped she hadn't thrown it out. She wanted the pleasure of that for herself.

She put her trainers on, managing to squeeze her bandaged foot in with care, and hobbled out of her room in search of the others, but the corridor outside didn't seem to lead anywhere except her room, a little sitting room and a room that looked like an office, so she went back through the door to the beautiful cloistered courtyard and looked around for any clues.

There were none.

So now what? She couldn't just stand there and yell, nor could she go round the courtyard systematically opening all the doors. Not that there were that many, but even so.

She was sitting there on the low wall around the central courtyard, studying the beautiful frescoes and trying to work out what to do if nobody showed up, when the door nearest to her opened and Massimo appeared. He'd showered and changed out of the suit into jeans and a soft white linen shirt stark against his olive skin, the cuffs rolled back to reveal those tanned forearms which had nearly been her undoing on the plane, and her heart gave a tiny lurch.

*Stupid.*

He caught sight of her and smiled, and her heart did another little jiggle as he walked towards her.

'Lydia, I was just coming to see if you were all right. I'm sorry, I should have come back quicker. How are you? How's the head?'

'Fine,' she said with a rueful smile. 'I'm just a

bit lost. I didn't want to go round opening all the doors, it seemed rude.'

'You should have shouted. I would have heard you.'

'I'm not in the habit of yelling for help,' she said drily, and he chuckled and came over to her side.

'Let me help you now,' he said, and offered her his arm. 'It's not far, hang on and hop, or would you rather I carried you?'

'I'll hop,' she said hastily, not sure she could cope with being snuggled up to that broad, solid chest again, with the feel of his arms strong and safe under her. 'I don't want to break you.'

He laughed at that. 'I don't think you'll break me. Did you find everything you needed? How's your room?'

She slipped her arm through his, conscious of the smell of him again, refreshed now by his shower and overlaid with soap and more of the citrusy cologne that had been haunting her nostrils all day. She wanted to press her nose to his chest, to breathe him in, to absorb the warmth and scent and maleness of him.

*Not* appropriate. She forced herself to concentrate.

'Lovely. The bath was utter bliss. I can't tell you how wonderful it was to get out of that awful dress. I hope Carlotta hasn't burned it, I want to do it myself.'

He laughed again, a warm, rich sound that echoed round the courtyard, and scanned her body with his eyes. 'It really didn't do you justice,' he said softly, and in the gentle light she thought she caught a glimpse of whatever it was she'd seen in his eyes at the airport.

But then it was gone, and he was opening the door and ushering her through to a big, brightly lit kitchen. Carlotta was busy at the stove, and the children were seated at a large table in the middle of the room, Antonino kneeling up and leaning over to interfere with what Lavinia was doing.

She pushed him aside crossly, and Massimo intervened before a fight could break out, diffusing it swiftly by splitting them up. While he was busy, Carlotta came and helped her to the table. She smiled at her gratefully.

'I'm sorry to put you to so much trouble.'

'Is no trouble,' she said. 'Sit, sit. Is ready.'

She sniffed, and smiled. 'It smells wonderful.'

'*Buono.* You eat, then you feel better. Sit!'

She flapped her apron at Lydia, and she sat obediently at the last place laid at the long table. It was opposite Francesca, and Massimo was at the end of the table on her right, bracketed by the two younger ones who'd been split up to stop them squabbling.

They were fractious—overtired, she thought guiltily, and missing their father. But Francesca was watching her warily. She smiled at the girl apologetically.

'I'm sorry I kept your father away from you for so long. He's been so kind and helpful.'

'He is. He helps everybody. Are you better now?'

'I'm all right. I've just got a bit of a headache but I don't think it's much more than that. I was so stupid. I tripped over the hem of my dress and fell down the steps of the plane and hit my head.'

Behind her, there was a clatter, and Francesca went chalk white, her eyes huge with horror and distress.

*'Scusami,'* she mumbled, and pushing back her chair, she ran from the room, her father following, his chair crashing over as he leapt to his feet.

'Francesca!' He reached the door before it

closed, and she could hear his voice calling as he ran after her. Horrified, uncertain what she'd done, she turned to Carlotta and found her with her apron pressed to her face, her eyes above it creased with distress.

'What did I say?' she whispered, conscious of the little ones, but Carlotta just shook her head and picked up the pan and thrust it in the sink.

'Is nothing. Here, eat. Antonino!'

He sat down, and Lavinia put away the book he'd been trying to tug away from her, and Carlotta picked up Massimo's overturned chair and ladled food out onto all their plates.

There was fresh bread drizzled with olive oil, and a thick, rich stew of beans and sausage and gloriously red tomatoes. It smelt wonderful, tasted amazing, but Lydia could scarcely eat it. The children were eating. Whatever it was she'd said or done had gone right over their heads, but something had driven Francesca from the room, and her father after her.

The same something that had made Massimo go pale at the airport, as he'd knelt on the tarmac at her side? The same something that had made him stand, rigid with tension, staring grimly at a poster when he thought she was asleep in the room at the hospital?

She pushed back her chair and hopped over to the sink, where Carlotta was scrubbing furiously at a pot. 'I'm sorry, I can't eat. Carlotta, what did I say?' she asked under her breath, and those old, wise eyes that had seen so much met hers, and she shook her head, twisting her hands in the dish-cloth and biting her lips.

She put the pot on the draining board, and Lydia automatically picked up a tea towel and dried it, her hip propped against the edge of the sink unit as she balanced on her good leg. Another pot followed, and another, and finally Carlotta stopped scouring the pots as if they were lined with demons and her hands came to rest.

She hobbled over to the children, cleared up their plates, gave them pudding and then gathered them up like a mother hen.

'Wait here. Eat. He will come back.'

They left her there in the kitchen, their footsteps echoing along a corridor and up stairs, and Lydia sank down at the table and stared blankly at the far wall, going over and over her words in her head and getting nowhere.

Carlotta appeared again and put Francesca's supper in a microwave.

'Is she coming down again? I want to apologise for upsetting her.'

'No. Is all right, *signorina*. Her *pàpa* look after her.' And lifting the plate out of the microwave, she carried it out of the room on a tray, leaving Lydia alone again.

She poked at her food, but it was cold now, the beans congealing in the sauce, and she ripped up a bit of bread and dabbed it absently in the stew. What had she said, that had caused such distress?

She had no idea, but she couldn't leave the kitchen without finding out, and there was still a pile of washing up to do. She didn't know where anything lived, but the table was big enough to put it all on, and there was a dishwasher sitting there empty.

Well, if she could do nothing else while she waited, she could do that, she told herself, and pushing up her sleeves, she hopped over to the dishwasher and set about clearing up the kitchen.

He had to go down to her—to explain, or apologise properly, at the very least.

His stomach growled, but he ignored it. He couldn't eat, not while his daughter was just settling into sleep at last, her sobs fading quietly away into the night.

He closed his eyes. Talking to Lydia, dredging it all up again, was the last thing he wanted to do, the very last, but he had no choice. Leaning over Francesca, he pressed a kiss lightly against her cheek, and straightened. She was sleeping peacefully now; he could leave her.

Leave her, and go and find Lydia, if she hadn't had the sense to pack up her things and leave. It seemed unlikely, but he couldn't blame her.

He found her in the kitchen, sitting with Carlotta over a cup of coffee, the kitchen sparkling. He stared at them, then at the kitchen. Carlotta had been upstairs until a short while ago, settling the others, and the kitchen had been in chaos, so how?

'She's OK now,' he said in Italian. 'Why don't you go to bed, Carlotta? You look exhausted and Roberto's worried about you.'

She nodded and got slowly to her feet, then rested her hand on Lydia's shoulder and patted it before leaving her side. 'I *am* tired,' she said to him in Italian, 'but you need to speak to Lydia.

I couldn't leave her. She's a good girl, Massimo. Look at my kitchen! A good, kind girl, and she's unhappy. Worried.'

He sighed. 'I know. Did you explain?'

'No. It's not my place, but be gentle with her—and yourself.' And with that pointed remark, she left them alone together.

Lydia looked up at him and searched his eyes. 'What did she say to you?'

He gave her a fleeting smile. 'She told me you were a good, kind girl. And she told me to be gentle with you.'

Her eyes filled, and she looked away. 'I don't know what I said, but I'm so, so sorry.'

His conscience pricked him. He should have warned her. He sighed and scrubbed a hand through his hair.

'No. I should be apologising, not you. Forgive us, we aren't normally this rude to visitors. Francesca was upset.'

'I know that. Obviously I made it happen. What I don't know is why,' she said, looking up at him again with grief-stricken eyes.

He reached for a mug, changed his mind and poured himself a glass of wine. 'Can I tempt you?'

'Is it one of yours?'

'No. It's a neighbour's, but it's good. We could take it outside. I don't know if it's wise, though, with your head injury.'

'I'll take the risk,' she said. 'And then will you tell me what I said?'

'You know what you said. What you don't know is what it meant,' he said enigmatically, and picking up both glasses of wine, he headed for the door, glancing back over his shoulder at her. 'Can you manage, or should I carry you?'

Carry her? With her face pressed up against that taunting aftershave, and the feel of his strong, muscled arms around her legs? 'I can manage,' she said hastily, and pushing back her chair, she got to her feet and limped after him out into the still, quiet night.

She could hear the soft chirr of insects, the sound of a motorbike somewhere in the valley below, and then she saw a single headlight slicing through the night, weaving and turning as it followed the snaking road along the valley bottom and disappeared.

He led her to a bench at the edge of the terrace. The ground fell away below them so it felt as if they were perched on the edge of the world, and when she was seated he handed her the glass and sat beside her, his elbows propped on his knees, his own glass dangling from his fingers as he stared out over the velvet blackness.

For a while neither of them said anything, but then the tension got to her and she broke the silence.

'Please tell me.'

He sucked in his breath, looking down, staring into his glass as he slowly swirled the wine before lifting it to his lips.

'Massimo?' she prompted, and he turned his head and met her eyes. Even in the moonlight, she could see the pain etched into his face, and her heart began to thud slowly.

'Angelina died of a brain haemorrhage following a fall,' he began, his voice expressionless. 'Nothing serious, nothing much at all, just a bit of a bump. She'd fallen down the stairs and hit her head on the wall. We all thought she was all right, but she had a bit of a headache later in the day, and we went to bed early. I woke in the night and she was missing, and I found her in the kitchen, slumped over the table, and one side of her face had collapsed.'

Lydia closed her eyes and swallowed hard as the nausea threatened to choke her. What had she *done*? Not just by saying what she had at the table—the same table? But by bringing this on all of them, on Claire, on him, on the children—most especially little Francesca, her eyes wide with pain and shock, fleeing from the table. The image would stay with her forever.

'It wasn't your fault,' he said gently. 'You weren't to know. I probably should have told you—warned you not to talk about it in that way, and why. I let you walk right into it.'

She turned back to him, searching his face in the shadows. She'd known something was wrong when he was bending over her on the tarmac, and again later, staring at the poster. And yet he'd said nothing.

'Why didn't you *tell* me? I knew something was wrong, something else, something more. Luca seemed much more worried than my condition warranted, even I knew that, and he kept looking at you anxiously. I thought he was worried about me, but then I realised it was you he was worried about. I just didn't know why. You should have told me.'

'How could I? You had a head injury. How could I say to you, "I'm sorry, I'm finding this a bit hard to deal with, my wife died of the same thing and I'm a bit worried I might lose you, too." How could I say that?'

*He'd been worried he could lose her?*

No. Of course he hadn't meant that, he didn't know her. He meant he was worried she might be about to die, too. Nothing more than that.

'You should have left us there instead of staying and getting distressed. I had no business tangling you all up in this mess—oh, Massimo, I'm so sorry.'

She broke off, clamping her teeth hard to stop her eyes from welling over, but his warm hand on her shoulder was the last straw, and she felt the hot, wet slide of a tear down her cheek.

'*Cara*, no. Don't cry for us. It was a long time ago.'

'But it still hurts you, and it'll hurt you forever,' she said unevenly.

'No, it just brought the memories back. We're all right, really. We're getting there. Francesca's the oldest, she remembers Angelina the most clearly, and she's the one who bears the brunt of the loss, because when I'm not there the little ones turn to her. She has to be mother to them, and she's been so strong, but she's just a little girl herself.'

He broke off, his jaw working, and she laid her hand gently against it and sighed.

'I'm so sorry. It must have been dreadful for you all.'

'It was. They took her to hospital, and she died later that day—she was on life support and they tested her brain but there was nothing. No activity at all. They turned off the machine, and I came home and told the children that their mother was gone. That was the hardest thing I've ever had to do in my life.'

His voice broke off again, turning away this time, and Lydia closed her eyes and swallowed the anguished response. There was nothing she could say that wouldn't be trite or meaningless, and so she stayed silent, and after a moment he let out a long, slow breath and sat back against the bench.

'So, now you know,' he said, his voice low and oddly flat.

Wordlessly, she reached out and touched his

hand, and he turned it, his fingers threading through hers and holding on tight.

They stayed like that for an age, their hands lying linked between them as they sipped their wine, and then he turned to her in the dim light and searched her face. He'd taken comfort from her touch, felt the warmth of her generous spirit seeping into him, easing the ache which had been a part of him for so long.

How could she do that with just a touch?

No words. Words were too hard, would have been trite. Did she know that?

Yes. He could see that she did, that this woman who talked too much actually knew the value of silence.

He lifted her hand and pressed it to his lips, then smiled at her sadly. 'Did you eat anything?'

She shook her head. 'No. Not really.'

'Nor did I. Shall we see what we can find? It's a very, very long time since breakfast.'

It wasn't exactly *haute cuisine*, but the simple fare of olive bread and ham and cheese with sweetly scented baby plum tomatoes and a bowl of olive oil and balsamic vinegar just hit the spot.

He poured them another glass of wine, but it didn't seem like a good idea and so she gave him the second half and he found some sparkling water for her. She realised she'd thought nothing of handing him her glass of wine for him to finish, and he'd taken it without hesitation and drunk from it without turning a hair.

How odd, when they'd only met a scant twelve hours ago. Thirteen hours and a few minutes, to be more exact.

It seemed more like a lifetime since she'd watched him getting out of the taxi, wondered if he'd be The One to make it happen. The guy she'd been talking to was funny and seemed nice enough, but he wasn't about to give her a lift and she knew that. But Massimo had looked at her as he'd gone into the Jet Centre foyer, his eyes meeting hers and locking…

She glanced up, and found him watching her with a frown.

'Why are you frowning?' she asked, and his mouth kicked up a fraction in one corner, the frown ironed out with a deliberate effort.

'No reason. How's your head now?'

She shrugged. 'OK. It just feels as if I fell over

my feet and spent the day hanging about in a hospital.' It was rather worse than that, but he didn't need to know about every ache and pain. The list was endless.

She reached out and covered his hand. 'Massimo, I'm all right,' she said softly, and the little frown came back.

'Sorry. It's just a reflex. I look after people—it's part of my job description. Everyone comes to me with their problems.'

She smiled at him, remembering her conversation with Francesca.

*'I'm sorry I kept your father away from you for so long. He's been so kind and helpful.'*

*'He is. He helps everybody.'*

'You're just a fixer, aren't you? You fix everything for everybody all the time, and you hate it when things can't be fixed.'

His frown deepened for a moment, and then he gave a wry laugh and pulled his hand away, swirling the wine in her glass before draining it. 'Is it so obvious?'

She felt her lips twitch. 'Only if you're on the receiving end. Don't get me wrong, I'm massively grateful and just so sorry I've dragged you into this awful mess and upset everyone. I'm more than happy you're a fixer, because goodness only knows I seemed to need one today. I think I need a guardian angel, actually. I just have such a gift for getting into a mess and dragging everybody with me.'

She broke off, and he tipped his head on one side and that little crease between his eyebrows returned fleetingly. 'A gift?'

She sighed. 'Jen's accident was sort of my fault.'

He sat back, his eyes searching hers. 'Tell me,' he said softly, so she did.

She told him about Russell, about their trip to her parents' farm for the weekend, because Jen and Andy were going to be there as well and she hadn't seen them for a while. And she'd shown him the farm, and he'd seen the quad bike, and suggested they went out on it so she could show him all the fields.

'I didn't want to go with him. He was a crazy driver, and I knew he'd want to go too fast, so I said no, but then Jen offered to show him round. She wanted to get him alone, to threaten him with death if he hurt me, but he hurt her instead. He went far too fast, and she told him to stop but he thought she was just being chicken and she wasn't, she knew about the fallen tree hidden in the long grass, and then they hit it and the quad bike cartwheeled through the air and landed on her.'

He winced and closed his eyes briefly. 'And she ended up in a wheelchair?'

'Not for a few weeks. She had a fractured spine, and she was in a special bed for a while. It wasn't displaced, the spinal cord wasn't severed but it was badly bruised and it took a long time to recover and for the bones to heal. She's getting better now, she's starting to walk again, but she lost her job and so did Andy, so he could look after her. He took away everything from them, and if I'd gone with him, if it had been me, then I might have been able to stop him.'

'You really think so? He sounds like an idiot.'

'He is an idiot,' she said tiredly. 'He's an idiot, and he was my boss, so I lost my job, too.'

'He sacked you?'

She gave him a withering look. 'I walked… and then his business folded without me, and he threatened to sue me if I didn't go back. I told him to take a flying hike.'

'What business was he in?'

'He had a restaurant. I was his chef.'

Hence the tidy kitchen, he realised. She was used to working in a kitchen, used to bringing order to chaos, used to the utensils and the work space and the arrangement of them that always to him defied logic. And his restaurant had folded without her?

'You told me you were a cook,' he rebuked her mildly. 'I didn't realise you were a chef.'

She quirked an eyebrow at him mockingly. 'You told me you were a farmer and you live in a flipping fortress! I think that trumps it,' she said drily, and he laughed and lifted his glass to her.

*'Touché,'* he said softly, and her heart turned over at the wry warmth in his eyes. 'I'm sorry,' he went on. 'Sorry about this man who clearly didn't deserve you, sorry about your sister, sorry about your job. What a mess. And all because he was a fool.'

'Absolutely.'

'Tell me more about him.'

'Like what?'

'Like why your sister felt she needed to warn him not to hurt you. Had you been hurt before?'

'No, but she didn't really like him. He wasn't always a nice man, and he took advantage of me—made me work ridiculous hours, treated me like a servant at times and yet he could be a charmer, too. He was happy enough to talk me into his bed once he realised I was a good chef—sorry, you really didn't need to know that.'

He smiled slightly. 'Maybe you needed to say it,' he suggested, and her laugh was a little brittle.

'There are so many things I could tell you about him. I said I was a lousy judge of character. I think he had a lot in common with Nico, perhaps.'

He frowned. 'Nico?'

'The guy at the airport?'

'Yes, I know who you mean. In what way? Was he a drinker?'

'Yes. Definitely. But not just a drinker. He was a nasty drunk, especially towards the end of our relationship. He seemed to change. Got arrogant. He used to be quite charming at first, but it was just a front. He—well, let's just say he didn't respect women either.'

His mouth tightened. 'I'm sorry. You shouldn't have had to tolerate that.'

'No, I shouldn't. So—tell me about your house,' she said, changing the subject to give them both a bit of a break. She reached out and tore off another strip of bread, dunking it in the oil that she couldn't get enough of, and looked up to see a strange look on his face. Almost—tender?

Nonsense. She was being silly. 'Well, come on, then,' she mumbled round the bread, and he smiled, the strange look disappearing as if she'd imagined it.

'It's very old. We're not sure of the origins. It seems it might have been a Medici villa, but the history is a little cloudy. It was built at the time of the Florentine invasion.'

'So how come your family ended up with it?'

His mouth twitched. 'One of our ancestors took possession of it at the end of the seventeenth century.'

That made her laugh. 'Took possession?'

The twitch again, and a wicked twinkle in his eye. 'We're not quite sure how he acquired it, but it's been in the family ever since. He's the one who renamed the villa *Palazzo Valtieri*.'

*Palazzo?* She nearly laughed at that. Not just a fortress, then, but a proper, full-on palace. Oh, boy.

'I'll show you round it tomorrow. It's beautiful.

Some of the frescoes are amazing, and the formal rooms in the part my parents live in are fantastic.'

'Your parents live here?' she asked, puzzled, because there'd been no mention of them. Not that they'd really had time, but—

'*Si*. It's a family business. They're away at the moment, snatching a few days with my sister Carla and her new baby before the harvest starts, but they'll be back the day after tomorrow.'

'So how many rooms are there?'

He laughed. 'I have no idea. I've never counted them, I'm too busy trying not to let it fall down. It's crumbling as fast as we can patch it up, but so long as we can cheat time, that's fine. It's quite interesting.'

'I'm sure it is. And now it's your turn to run it?'

His mouth tugged down at the corners, but there was a smile in his eyes. '*Si*. For my sins. My father keeps trying to interfere, but he's supposed to be retired. He doesn't understand that, though.'

'No. It must be hard to hand it over. My father wouldn't be able to do it. And the harvest is just starting?'

He nodded. 'The grape harvest is first, followed by the chestnuts and the olives. It's relentless now until the end of November, so you can see why I was in a hurry to get back.'

'And I held you up.'

'*Cara*, accidents happen. Don't think about it any more.' He pushed back his chair. 'I think it's time you went to bed. It's after midnight.'

Was it? When had that happened? When they were outside, sitting in the quiet of the night and watching the twinkling lights in the villages? Or now, sitting here eating bread and cheese and olive oil, drinking wine and staring into each other's eyes like lovers?

She nodded and pushed back her chair, and he tucked her arm in his so she could feel the solid muscle of his forearm under her hand, and she hung on him and hopped and hobbled her way to her room.

'Ring me if you need anything. You have my mobile number on my card. I gave it to you on the plane. Do you still have it?'

'Yes—but I won't need you.'

Well, not for anything she'd dream of asking him for…

His brows tugged together. 'Just humour me, OK? If you feel unwell in the night, or want anything, ring me and I'll come down. I'm not far away. And please, don't lock your door.'

'Massimo, I'm feeling all right. My headache's gone, and I feel OK now. You don't need to worry.'

'You can't be too careful,' he said, and she could see a tiny frown between his brows, as if he was still waiting for something awful to happen to her.

They reached her room and he paused at the door, staring down into her eyes and hesitating for the longest moment. And then, just when she thought he was going to kiss her, he stepped back.

'Call me if you need me. If you need anything at all.'

'I will.'

'Good. *Buonanotte*, Lydia,' he murmured softly, and turned and walked away.

# CHAPTER FOUR

WHAT was she *thinking* about?

Of course he hadn't been about to kiss her! That bump on the head had obviously been more serious than she'd realised. Maybe a blast of fresh air would help her think clearly?

She opened the French doors onto the terrace and stood there for a moment, letting the night air cool her heated cheeks. She'd been so carried along on the moment, so lured by his natural and easy charm that she'd let herself think all sorts of stupid things.

Of course he wasn't interested in her. Why would he be? She'd been nothing but a thorn in his side since the moment he'd set eyes on her. And even if he hadn't, she wasn't interested! Well, that was a lie, of course she was interested, or she wouldn't even be thinking about it, but there was no way it was going anywhere.

Not after the debacle with Russell. She was

sworn off men now for life, or at least for a good five years. And so far, it hadn't been much more than five months!

Leaving the doors open, she limped back to the bed and pulled her pyjamas out of her flight bag, eyeing them dubiously. The skimpy top and little shorts she'd brought for their weightlessness had seemed fine when she was going to be sharing a hotel room with Claire, but here, in this ancient historic house—*palazzo*, even, for heaven's sake! She wondered what on earth he'd make of them.

Nothing. Nothing at all, because he wasn't going to see her in her nightclothes! Cross with herself, her head aching and her ankle throbbing and her bruises giving her a fair amount of grief as well, she changed into the almost-pyjamas, cleaned her teeth and crawled into bed.

Oh, bliss. The pillows were cloud-soft, the down quilt light and yet snuggly, and the breeze from the doors was drifting across her face, bringing with it the scents of sage and lavender and night-scented stocks.

Exhausted, weary beyond belief, she closed her eyes with a little sigh and drifted off to sleep…

* * *

Her doors were open.

He hesitated, standing outside on the terrace, questioning his motives.

Did he *really* think she needed checking in the night? Or was he simply indulging his—what? Curiosity? Fantasy? Or, perhaps…need?

He groaned softly. There was no doubt that he *needed* her, needed the warmth of her touch, the laughter in her eyes, the endless chatter and the brilliance of her smile.

The silence, when she'd simply held his hand and offered comfort.

Thinking about that moment brought a lump to his throat, and he swallowed hard. He hadn't allowed himself to need a woman for years, but Lydia had got under his skin, penetrated his defences with her simple kindness, and he wanted her in a way that troubled him greatly, because it was more than just physical.

And he really wasn't sure he was ready for that—would ever be ready for that again. But the need…

He'd just check on her, just to be on the safe side. He couldn't let her lie there alone all night.

Not like Angelina.

Guilt crashed over him again, driving out the need and leaving sorrow in its wake. Focused now, he went into her room, his bare feet silent on the tiled floor, and gave his eyes a moment to adjust to the light.

Had she sensed him? Maybe, because she sighed and shifted, the soft, contented sound drifting to him on the night air. When had he last heard a woman sigh softly in her sleep?

Too long ago to remember, too soon to forget.

It would be so easy to reach out his hand, to touch her. To take her in his arms, warm and sleepy, and make love to her.

Easy, and yet impossibly wrong. What was it about her that made him feel like this, that made him think things he hadn't thought in years? Not since he'd lost Angelina.

He stood over her, staring at her in the moonlight, the thought of his wife reminding him of why he was here. Not to watch Lydia sleep, like some kind of voyeur, but to keep her safe. He focused on her face. It was peaceful, both sides the same, just as it had been when he'd left her for the night, and she was breathing slowly and evenly.

As he watched she moved her arms, pushing the covers lower. Both arms, both working.

He swallowed. She was fine, just as she'd told him, he realised in relief. He could go to bed now, relax.

But it was too late. He'd seen her sleeping, heard that soft, feminine sigh and the damage was done. His body, so long denied, had come screaming back to life, and he wouldn't sleep now.

Moving carefully so as not to disturb her, he made his way back to the French doors and out onto the terrace. Propping his hands on his hips, he dropped his head back and sucked in a lungful of cool night air, then let it out slowly before dragging his hand over his face.

He'd swim. Maybe that would take the heat out of his blood. And if it was foolish to swim alone, if he'd told the children a thousand times that no one should ever do it—well, tonight was different.

Everything about tonight seemed different.

He crossed the upper terrace, padded silently down the worn stone steps to the level below and rolled back the thermal cover on the pool. The water was warm, steaming billowing from the surface in the cool night air, and stripping off his clothes, he dived smoothly in.

Something had woken her.

She opened her eyes a fraction, peeping through the slit between her eyelids, but she could see nothing.

She could hear something, though. Not loud, just a little, rhythmic splash—like someone swimming?

She threw off the covers and sat up, wincing a little as her head pounded and the bruises twinged with the movement. She fingered the egg on her head, and sighed. *Idiot.* First thing in the morning she was going to track down that dress and burn the blasted thing.

She inched to the edge of the bed, and stood up slowly, her ankle protesting as she put weight through it. Not as badly as yesterday, though, she thought, and limped out onto the terrace to listen for the noise.

Yes. Definitely someone swimming. And it seemed to be coming from straight ahead. As she felt her way cautiously across the stone slabs and then the grass, she realised that this was the terrace they'd sat on last night, or at least a part of it. They'd been further over, to her left, and straight ahead of her were railings, the top edge gleaming in the moonlight.

She made her way slowly to them and looked down, and there he was. Well, there someone was, slicing through the water with strong, bold strokes, up and down, up and down, length after length through the swirling steam that rose from the surface of the pool.

Exorcising demons?

Then finally he slowed, rolled to his back and floated spread-eagled on the surface. She could barely make him out because the steam clouded the air in the moonlight, but she knew instinctively it was him.

And as if he'd sensed her, he turned his head and as the veil of mist was drawn back for an instant, their eyes met in the night. Slowly, with no sense of urgency, he swam to the side, folded his arms and rested on them, looking up at her.

'You're awake.'

'Something woke me, then I heard the splashing. Is it sensible to swim on your own in the dark?'

He laughed softly. 'You could always come in. Then I wouldn't be alone.'

'I haven't got any swimming things.'

'Ah. Well, that's probably not very wise then because neither have I.'

She sucked in her breath softly, and closed her eyes, suddenly embarrassed. Amongst other things. 'I'm sorry. I didn't realise. I'll go away.'

'Don't worry, I'm finished. Just close your eyes for a second so I don't offend you while I get out.'

She heard the laughter in his voice, then the sound of him vaulting out of the pool. Her eyes flew open, and she saw him straighten up, water sluicing off his back as he walked calmly to a sun lounger and picked up an abandoned towel. He dried himself briskly as she watched, unable to look away, mesmerised by those broad shoulders that tapered down to lean hips and powerful legs.

In the magical silver light of the moon, the taut, firm globes of his buttocks, paler than the rest of him, could have been carved from marble, like one of the statues that seemed to litter the whole of Italy. Except they'd be warm, of course, alive…

Her mouth dry, she snapped her eyes shut again

and made herself breath. In, out, in, out, nice and slowly, slowing down, calmer.

'Would you like a drink?'

She jumped and gave a tiny shriek. 'Don't creep up on people like that!' she whispered fiercely, and rested her hand against the pounding heart beneath her chest.

Yikes. Her all but bare chest, in the crazily insubstantial pyjamas…

'I'm not really dressed for entertaining,' she mumbled, which was ridiculous because the scanty towel twisted round his hips left very little to the imagination.

His fingers, cool and damp, appeared under her chin, tilting her head up so she could see his face instead of just that tantalising towel. His eyes were laughing.

'That makes two of us. I tell you what, I'll go and put the kettle on and pull on my clothes, and you go and find something a little less…'

'Revealing?'

His smile grew crooked. 'I was going to say alluring.'

Alluring. Right.

'I'll get dressed,' she said hastily, and limped

rather faster than was sensible back towards her room, shutting the doors firmly behind her.

He watched her hobble away, his eyes tracking her progress across the terrace in the skimpiest of pyjamas, the long slender legs that had been hidden until now revealed by those tiny shorts in a way that did nothing for his peace of mind.

Or the state of his body. He swallowed hard and tightened his grip on the towel.

So much for the swimming cooling him down, he thought wryly, and went into the kitchen through the side door, rubbed himself briskly down with the towel again and pulled on his clothes, then switched on the kettle. Would she be able to find him? Would she even know which way to go?

Yes. She was there, in the doorway, looking deliciously rumpled and sleepy and a little uncertain. She'd pulled on her jeans and the T-shirt she'd been wearing last night, and her unfettered breasts had been confined to a bra. Pity, he thought, and then chided himself. She was a guest in his house, she was injured, and all he could do was lust after her. He should be ashamed of himself.

'Tea, coffee or something else? I expect there are some herbal teabags or something like that.'

'Camomile?' she asked hopefully.

Something to calm her down, because her host, standing there in bare feet, a damp T-shirt clinging to the moisture on his chest and a pair of jeans that should have had a health warning on them hanging on his lean hips was doing nothing for her equilibrium.

Not now she knew what was underneath those clothes.

He poured boiling water into a cup for her, then stuck another cup under the coffee maker and pressed a button. The sound of the grinding beans was loud in the silence, but not loud enough to drown out the sound of her heartbeat.

She should have stayed in her room, kept out of his way.

'Here, I don't know how long you want to keep the teabag in.'

He put the mug down on the table and turned back to the coffee maker, and as she stirred the teabag round absently she watched him. His hands were deft, his movements precise as he spooned sugar and stirred in a splash of milk.

'Won't that keep you awake?' she asked, but he just laughed softly.

'It's not a problem, I'm up now for the day. After I've drunk this I'll go and tackle some work in my office, and then I'll have breakfast with the children before I go out and check the grapes in each field to see if they're ripe.'

'Has the harvest started?'

*'La vendemmia?'* He shook his head. 'No. If the grapes are ripe, it starts tomorrow. We'll spend the rest of the day making sure we're ready, because once it starts, we don't stop till it's finished. But today—today should be pretty routine.'

So he might have time to show her round…

'Want to come with me and see what we do? If you're interested, of course. Don't feel you have to.'

If she was interested? She nearly laughed. *The farm,* she told herself firmly. He was talking about the *farm*.

'That would be great, if I won't be in your way?'

'No, of course not. It might be dull, though, and once I leave the house I won't be back for hours. I don't know if you're feeling up to it.'

Was he trying to get out of it? Retracting his

invitation, thinking better of having her hanging around him all day like a stray kitten that wouldn't leave him alone?

'I can't walk far,' she said, giving him a get-out clause, but he shook his head.

'No, you don't have to. We'll take the car, and if you don't feel well I can always bring you back, it's not a problem.'

That didn't sound as if he was trying to get out of it, and she was genuinely interested.

'It sounds great. What time do you want to leave?'

'Breakfast is at seven. We'll go straight afterwards.'

It was fascinating.

He knew every inch of his land, every nook and cranny, every slope, every vine, almost, and as he stood on the edge of a little escarpment pointing things out to her, his feet planted firmly in the soil, she thought she'd never seen anyone who belonged so utterly to their home.

He looked as if he'd grown from the very soil beneath his feet, his roots stretching down into it for three hundred years. It was a part of him, and he was a part of it, the latest guardian in its history, and it was clear that he took the privilege incredibly seriously.

As they drove round the huge, sprawling estate to check the ripeness of the grapes on all the slopes, he told her about each of the grape varieties which grew on the different soils and orientations, lifting handfuls of the soil so she could see the texture, sifting it through his fingers as he talked about moisture content and pH levels and how it varied from field to field, and all the time his fingers were caressing the soil like a lover.

He mesmerised her.

Then he dropped the soil, brushed off his hands and gave her a wry smile.

'I'm boring you to death. Come on, it's time for lunch.'

He helped her back to the car, frowning as she trod on some uneven ground and gave a little cry as her ankle twisted.

'I'm sorry, it's too rough for you. Here.' And without hesitating he scooped her off her feet and set her back on the passenger seat, shut the door and went round and slid in behind the wheel.

He must have been mad to bring her out here

on the rough ground in the heat of the day, with a head injury and a sprained ankle. He hadn't been thinking clearly, what with the upset of yesterday and Francesca's scene at the table and then the utter distraction of her pyjamas—even if he'd been intending to go back to bed, there was no way he would have slept. In fact, he doubted if he'd ever sleep again!

He put her in the car, drove back to the villa and left her there with Carlotta. He'd been meaning to show her round the house, but frankly, even another moment in her company was too dangerous to contemplate at the moment.

He made a work-related excuse, and escaped.

He had a lot to do, he'd told her as he'd hurried off, because *la vendemmia* would start the following day.

So much for her tour of the house, she thought, but maybe it was as well to keep a bit of distance, because her feelings for him were beginning to confuse her.

Roberto brought the children home from school at the end of the afternoon, and she heard them splashing in the pool. She'd been contemplating the water herself, but without a suit it wasn't a goer, so she'd contented herself with sitting in the sun for a while and relaxing.

She went over to the railings and looked down, and saw all three of them in the water, with Carlotta and Roberto sitting in the shade watching them and keeping order. Carlotta glanced up at her and waved her down, and she limped down the steps and joined them.

It looked so inviting. Was her face a giveaway? Maybe, because Carlotta got to her feet and went to a door set in the wall of the terrace, under the steps. She emerged with a sleek black one-piece and offered it to her. 'Swim?' she said, encouragingly.

It was so, so tempting, and the children didn't seem to mind. Lavinia swam to the edge and grinned at her, and Antonino threw a ball at her and missed, and then giggled because she threw it back and bounced it lightly off his head. Only Francesca kept her distance, and she could understand why. It was the first time she'd seen her since supper last night, and maybe now she'd find a chance to apologise.

She changed in the cubicle Carlotta had taken

the costume from, and sat on the edge of the pool to take off her elastic ankle support.

'Ow. It looks sore.'

She glanced up, and saw Francesca watching her warily, her face troubled.

'I'm all right,' she assured her with a smile. 'I was really stupid to fall like that. I'm so sorry I upset you last night.'

She shrugged, and returned the smile with a tentative one of her own. 'Is OK. I was just tired, and *Pàpa* had been away for days, and—I'm OK. Sometimes, I just remember...'

She nodded, trying to understand what it must be like to be ten and motherless, and coming up with nothing even close, she was sure.

'I'm sorry.' She slipped into the water next to Francesca, and reached out and touched her shoulder gently. Then she smiled at her. 'I wonder, would you teach me some words of Italian?'

'Sure. What?'

'Just basic things. Sorry. Thank you. Hello, goodbye—just things like that.'

'Of course. Swim first, then I teach you.'

And she smiled, a dazzling, pretty smile like

the smile of her mother in the photograph, and it nearly broke Lydia's heart.

He came into the kitchen as she was sitting there with the children, Francesca patiently coaching her.

'No! *Mee dees-pya-che,*' said Francesca, and Lydia repeated it, stretching the vowels.

'That's good. *Ciao, bambini*!'

*'Ciao, Pàpa!'* the children chorused, and he came over and sat down with them.

'I'm teaching Lydia *Italiano*,' Francesca told him, grinning at him.

He smiled back, his eyes indulgent. *'Mia bella ragazza,'* he said softly, and her smile widened, a soft blush colouring her cheeks.

'So what do you know?' he asked Lydia, and she laughed ruefully.

'*Mi dispiace*—I thought sorry was a word I ought to master pretty early on, with my track record,' she said drily, and he chuckled.

'Anything else?'

'*Grazie mille*—I seem to need that a lot, too! And *per favore*, because it's rude not to say please. And *prego*, just in case I ever get the chance to do something that someone thanks me for. And that's it, so far, but I think it's the most critical ones.'

He laughed. 'It's a good start. Right, children, bedtime. Say goodnight.'

'*Buonanotte*, Lydia,' they chorused, and she smiled at them and said, *'Buonanotte,'* back.

And then she looked at Francesca, and added, '*Grazie mille*, Francesca,' her eyes soft, and Francesca smiled back.

'*Prego*. We do more tomorrow?'

*'Si.'*

She grinned, and then out of the blue she came over to Lydia and kissed her on both cheeks. 'Goodnight.'

'Goodnight, Francesca.'

He ushered them away, although Francesca didn't really need to go to bed this early, but she'd lost sleep the night before and she was always happy to lie in bed and read.

He chivvied them through the bathroom, checked their teeth, redid Antonino's and then tucked them up. As he bent to kiss Francesca goodnight, she slid her arms round his neck and hugged him. 'I like Lydia,' she said. 'She's nice.'

'She is nice,' he said. 'Thank you for helping her.'

'It's OK. How long is she staying?'

'I don't know. A few days, just until she's better. You go to sleep, now.'

He turned off her top light, leaving the bedside light on so she could read for a while, and went back down to the kitchen.

Lydia was sitting there studying an English-Italian dictionary that Francesca must have lent her, and he poured two glasses of wine and sat down opposite her.

'She's a lovely girl.'

'She is. She's very like her mother. Kind. Generous.'

Lydia nodded. 'I'm really sorry you lost her.'

He smiled, but said nothing. What was there to say? Nothing he hadn't said before.

'So, the harvest starts tomorrow,' Lydia said after a moment.

'*Si.* You should come down. Carlotta brings lunch for everyone at around twelve-thirty. Come with her, I'll show you what we do.'

Massimo left before dawn the following morning, and she found Carlotta up to her eyes in the kitchen.

'How many people are you feeding?' she asked.

Carlotta's face crunched up thoughtfully, and she said something in Italian which was meaningless, then held up her outspread hands and flashed them six times. Sixty. *Sixty?*

'Wow! That's a lot of work.'

'*Si*. Is lot of work.'

She looked tired at the very thought, and Lydia frowned slightly and began to help without waiting to be asked. They loaded the food into a truck at twelve, and Roberto, Carlotta's husband, drove them down to the centre of operations.

They followed the route she'd travelled with Massimo the day before, bumping along the gravelled road to a group of buildings. It was a hive of activity, small tractors and pickup trucks in convoy bringing in the grapes, a tractor and trailer with men and women crowded on the back laughing and joking, their spirits high.

Massimo met them there, and helped her down out of the truck with a smile. 'Come, I'll show you round,' he said, and led her to the production line.

Around the tractors laden with baskets of grapes, the air was alive with the hum of bees. Everyone was covered in sticky purple grape juice, the air heavy with sweat and the sweet scent of freshly pressed grapes, and over the sound of excited voices she could hear the noise of the motors powering the pumps and the pressing machines.

'It's fascinating,' she yelled, and he nodded.

'It is. You can stay, if you like, see what we do with the grapes.'

'Do you need me underfoot?' she asked, and his mouth quirked.

'I'm sure I'll manage. You ask intelligent questions. I can live with that.'

His words made her oddly happy, and she smiled. 'Thank you. They seem to be enjoying themselves,' she added, gesturing to the laughing workers, and he grinned.

'Why wouldn't they be? We all love the harvest. And anyway, it's lunchtime,' he said pragmatically as the machines fell silent, and she laughed.

'So it is. I'm starving.'

The lunch was just a cold spread of bread and cheese and ham and tomatoes, much like their impromptu supper in the middle of the first night, and the exhausted and hungry workers fell on it like locusts.

'Carlotta told me there are about sixty people to feed. Does she do this every day?'

'Yes—and an evening meal for everyone. It's too much for her, but she won't let anyone else take over, she insists on being in charge and she's so fussy about who she'll allow in her kitchen it's not easy to get help that she'll accept.'

She nodded. She could understand that. She'd learned the art of delegation, but you still had to have a handle on everything that was happening in the kitchen and that took energy and physical resources that Carlotta probably didn't have any more.

'How old is she?'

Massimo laughed. 'It's a state secret and more than my life's worth to reveal it. Roberto's eighty-two. She tells me it's none of my business, which makes it difficult as she's on the payroll, so I had to prise it out of Roberto. Let's just say there's not much between them.'

That made her chuckle, but it also made her think. Carlotta hadn't minded her helping out in the kitchen this morning, or the other night—in fact, she'd almost seemed grateful. Maybe she'd see if she could help that afternoon. 'I think I'll head back with them,' she told him. 'It's a bit hot out here for me now anyway, and I could do with putting my foot up for a while.'

It wasn't a lie, none of it, but she had no intention of putting her foot up if Carlotta would let her help. And it would be a way to repay them for all the trouble she'd caused.

It was an amazing amount of work.

It would have been a lot for a team. For Carlotta, whose age was unknown but somewhere in the ballpark of eighty-plus, it was ridiculous. She had just the one helper, Maria, who sighed with relief when Lydia offered her assistance.

So did Carlotta.

Oh, she made a fuss, protested a little, but more on the lines of 'Oh, you don't really want to,' rather than, 'No, thank you, I don't need your help.'

So she rolled up her sleeves and pitched in, peeling and chopping a huge pile of vegetables. Carlotta was in charge of browning the diced chicken, seasoning the tomato-based sauce, tasting.

That was fine. This was her show. Lydia was

just going along for the ride, and making up for the disaster of her first evening here, but by the time they were finished and ready to serve it on trestle tables under the cherry trees, her ankle was paying for it.

She stood on one leg like a stork, her sore foot hooked round her other calf, wishing she could sit down and yet knowing she was needed as they dished up to the hungry hordes.

They still looked happy, she thought. Happy and dirty and smelly and as if they'd had a good day, and there was a good deal of teasing and flirting going on, some of it in her direction.

She smiled back, dished up and wondered where Massimo was. She found herself scanning the crowd for him, and told herself not to be silly. He'd be with the children, not here, not eating with the workers.

She was wrong. A few minutes later, when the queue was thinning out and she was at the end of her tether, she felt a light touch on her waist.

'You should be resting. I'll take over.'

And his firm hands eased her aside, took the ladle from her hand and carried on.

'You don't need to do that. You've been working all day.'

'So have you, I gather, and you're hurt. Have you eaten?'

'No. I was waiting till we'd finished.'

He ladled sauce onto the last plate and turned to her. 'We're finished. Grab two plates, we'll go and eat. And you can put your foot up. You told me you were going to do that and I hear you've been standing all day.'

They sat at the end of a trestle, so she was squashed between a young girl from one of the villages and her host, and the air was heady with the scent of sweat and grape juice and the rich tomato and basil sauce.

He shaved cheese over her pasta, his arm brushing hers as he held it over her plate, and the soft chafe of hair against her skin made her nerve-endings dance.

'So, is it a good harvest?' she asked, and he grinned.

'Very good. Maybe the best I can remember. It'll be a vintage year for our Brunello.'

'Brunello? I thought that was only from Montalcino?'

'It is. Part of the estate is in the Montalcino territory. It's very strictly regulated, but it's a very important part of our revenue.'

'I'm sure.' She was. During the course of her training and apprenticeships she'd learned a lot about wines, and she knew that Brunellos were always expensive, some of them extremely so. Expensive, and exclusive. Definitely niche market.

Her father would be interested. He'd like Massimo, she realised. They had a lot in common, in so many ways, for all the gulf between them.

Deep in thought, she ate the hearty meal, swiped the last off the sauce from her plate with a chunk of bread and licked her lips, glancing up to see him watching her with a smile on his face.

'What?'

'You. You really appreciate food.'

'I do. Carlotta's a good cook. That was delicious.'

'Are you making notes?'

She laughed. 'Only mental ones.'

He glanced over her head, and a smile touched his face. 'My parents are back. They're looking forward to meeting you.'

Really? Like this, covered in tomato sauce and

reeking of chopped onions? She probably had an orange tide-line round her mouth, and her hair was dragged back into an elastic band, and—

'Mamma, *Pàpa*, this is Lydia.'

She scrambled to her feet, wincing as her sore ankle took her weight, and looked up into the eyes of an elegant, beautiful, immaculately groomed woman with clear, searching eyes.

'Lydia. How nice to meet you. Welcome to our home. I'm Elisa Valtieri, and this is my husband, Vittorio.'

'Hello. It's lovely to meet you, too.' Even if she did look a fright.

She shook their hands, Elisa's warm and gentle, Vittorio's rougher, his fingers strong and hard, a hand that wasn't afraid of work. He was an older version of his son, and his eyes were kind. He reminded her of her father.

'My son tells me you've had an accident?' Elisa said, her eyes concerned.

'Yes, I was really stupid, and he's been unbelievably kind.'

'And so, I think, have you. Carlotta is singing your praises.'

'Oh.' She felt herself colour, and laughed a little awkwardly. 'I didn't have anything else to do.'

'Except rest,' Massimo said drily, but his smile was gentle and warmed her right down to her toes.

And then she glanced back and found his mother looking at her, curiosity and interest in those lively brown eyes, and she excused herself, mumbling some comment about them having a lot to catch up on, and hobbled quickly back to Carlotta to see if there was anything she could do to help.

Anything, other than stand there while his mother eyed her speculatively, her eyes asking questions Lydia had no intention of answering.

If she even knew the answers…

# CHAPTER FIVE

'YOU ran away.'

She was sitting outside her room on a bench with her foot up, flicking through a magazine she'd found, and she looked up guiltily into his thoughtful eyes.

'I had to help Carlotta.'

'And it was easier than dealing with my mother,' he said softly, a fleeting smile in his eyes. 'I'm sorry, she can be a little…'

'A little…?'

He grinned slightly crookedly. 'She doesn't like me being on my own. Every time I speak to a woman under fifty, her radar picks it up. She's been interrogating me for the last three hours.'

Lydia laughed, and she put the magazine down, swung her foot to the ground and patted the bench. 'Want to hide here for a while?'

His mouth twitched. 'How did you guess? Give me a moment.'

He vanished, then reappeared with a bottle of wine and two glasses. 'Prosecco?'

'Lovely. Thanks.' She took a glass from him, sniffing the bubbles and wrinkling her nose as she sipped. 'Mmm, that's really nice. So, how was the baby?'

'Beautiful, perfect, amazing, the best baby in the world—oh, apart from all their other grandchildren. This is the sixth, and Luca and Isabelle are about to make it seven. Their second is due any time now.'

'Wow. Lots of babies.'

'Yes, and she loves it. Nothing makes her happier. Luca and Isabelle and my brother Gio are coming over tomorrow for dinner with some neighbours, by the way. I'd like you to join us, if you can tolerate it.'

She stared at him. 'Really? I'm only here by default, and I feel such a fraud. I really ought to go home.'

'How's your head now?'

She pulled a face. 'Better. I'm still getting the odd headache, but nothing to worry about. It's my ankle and the other bruises and scrapes that are sorest. I think I hit every step.'

He frowned. 'I'm sorry. I didn't really think about the things I can't see.'

Well, that was a lie. He thought about them all the time, but there was no way he was confessing that to Lydia. 'So—will you join us?'

She bit her lip, worrying it for a moment with her teeth, which made him want to kiss her just to stop her hurting that soft, full mouth that had been taunting him for days. *Dio*, the whole damn woman had been taunting him for days—

'Can I think about it?'

*A kiss?* No. No! Not a kiss!

'Of course,' he said, finally managing to unravel his tongue long enough to speak. 'Of course you may. It won't be anything impressive, Carlotta's got enough to do as it is, but my mother wanted to see Isabelle and Luca before the baby comes, and Gio's coming, and so my mother's invited Anita and her parents, and so it gets bigger—you know how it is.'

She laughed softly. 'I can imagine. Who's Anita?'

'The daughter of our neighbours. She and Gio

had a thing a while back, and my mother keeps trying to get them together again. Can't see it working, really, but she likes to try.'

'And how do they feel?'

He laughed abruptly. 'I wouldn't dare ask Gio. He has a fairly bitter and twisted attitude to love. Comes from being a lawyer, I suppose. His first line of defence is always a pre-nuptial agreement.'

She raised an eyebrow. 'Trust issues, then. I can understand that. I have a few of my own after Russell.'

'I'm sure. People like that can take away something precious, a sort of innocence, a naivety, and once it's gone you can never get it back. Although I have no idea what happened to Gio. He won't talk about it.'

'What about Anita? What's she like?'

His low chuckle made her smile. 'Anita's a wedding planner. What do you think?'

'I think she might like to plan her own?'

'Indeed. But Gio can't see what's under his nose, even if Mamma keeps putting her there.' He tipped his head on one side. 'It could be an interesting evening. And if you're there, it might take the heat off Gio, so he'll probably be so busy being grateful he'll forget to quiz me about you, so it could be better all round!'

She started to laugh at that, and he joined in with another chuckle and topped up her glass.

'Here's to families and their politics and complications,' he said drily, and touched his glass to hers.

'Amen to that,' she said, remembering guiltily that she'd meant to phone Jen again. 'I heard from Claire, by the way—she's back home safely, and she said Jo's ecstatic about winning.'

'How's your sister about it?'

She pulled a face. 'I'm not sure. She was putting on a brave face, but I think she's gutted. I know none of us expected me to win but, you know, it would have been so nice.'

He nodded. 'I'm sorry.'

'Don't be. You've done more than enough.' She drained her glass and handed it to him. 'I'm going to turn in. I need to rest my leg properly, and tomorrow I need to think about arranging a flight back home.'

'For tomorrow?' He sounded startled, and she shook her head.

'No. I thought maybe the next day? I probably

ought to phone the hospital and get the go-ahead to fly.'

'I can take you there if you want a check-up.'

'You've got so much to do.'

'Nothing that's more important,' he said, and although it wasn't true, she knew that for him there was nothing more important than making sure there wasn't another Angelina.

'I'll see what they say,' she compromised. There was always the bus, surely? She'd ask Carlotta in the morning.

She got to her feet, and he stood up and took her hand, tucking it in the crook of his arm and helping her to the French doors. Quite unnecessarily, since she'd been hobbling around without help since the second day, really, but it was still nice to feel the strength of his arm beneath her hand, the muscles warm and hard beneath the fine fabric of his shirt.

Silk and linen, she thought, sampling the texture with her fingertips, savouring it.

He hesitated at the door, and then just when she thought he was going to walk away, he lowered his head and touched his lips to hers, sending rivers of ice and fire dancing over her skin.

It was a slow kiss, lingering, thoughtful, their mouths the only point of contact, but then the velvet stroke of his tongue against her lips made her gasp softly and part them for him, and everything changed.

He gave a muffled groan and deepened the kiss, searching the secret recesses of her mouth, his tongue finding hers and dancing with it, retreating, tangling, coaxing until she thought her legs would collapse.

Then he eased away, breaking the contact so slowly so that for a tiny second their lips still clung.

'*Buonanotte*, Lydia,' he murmured unevenly, his breath warm against her mouth, and then straightening slowly, he took a step back and turned briskly away, gathering up the glasses and the bottle as he went without a backwards glance.

She watched him go, then closed the curtains and undressed, leaving the doors open. The night was warm still, the light breeze welcome, and she lay there in the darkness, her fingertips tracing her lips, and thought about his kiss…

He must have been mad to kiss her!

Crazy. Insane. If he hadn't walked away, he

would have taken her right there, standing on the terrace in full view of anyone who walked past.

He headed for the stairs, but then hesitated. He wouldn't sleep—but what else could he do? His office was next to her room, and he didn't trust himself that close to her. The pool, his first choice of distraction for the sheer physical exertion it offered, was too close to her room, and she slept with her doors open. She'd hear him, come and investigate, and…

So not the pool, then.

Letting out a long, weary sigh, he headed slowly up the stairs to his room, and sat on the bed, staring at the photograph of Angelina on his bedside table.

He'd loved her—really, deeply and enduringly loved her. But she was gone, and now, as he looked at her face, another face seemed superimposed on it, a face with laughing eyes and a soft, full bottom lip that he could still taste.

He groaned and fell back against the pillows, staring up at the ceiling. The day after tomorrow, she'd be gone, he told himself, and then had to deal with the strange and unsettling sense of loss he felt at the thought that he was about to lose her.

* * *

She didn't sleep well.

Her dreams had been vivid and unsettling, and as soon as she heard signs of life, she got up, showered and put on her rinsed-out underwear, and then sat down on the edge of the bed and sighed thoughtfully as she studied her clothes.

She couldn't join them for dinner—not if their neighbours were coming. She'd seen Elisa, seen the expensive and elegant clothes she'd worn for travelling back home from her daughter's house, and the only things she had with her were the jeans and top she'd been wearing now for two days, including all the cooking she'd done yesterday.

No way could she wear them to dinner, even if she'd earn Gio's undying gratitude and give Elisa something else to think about! She put the clothes on, simply because she had absolutely no choice apart from the wedding dress Carlotta had stuffed in a bag for her and which she yet had to burn, and went outside and round the corner to the kitchen.

Carlotta was there, already making headway on the lunch preparations, and the children were sitting at the table eating breakfast. For a slightly crazy moment, she wondered if they could tell what she'd been dreaming about, if the fact that she'd kissed their father was written all over her face.

She said good morning to them, in her best Italian learned yesterday from Francesca, asked them how they were and then went over to Carlotta. '*Buongiorno*, Carlotta,' she said softly, and Carlotta blushed and smiled at her and patted her cheek.

'*Buongiorno, signorina,*' she said. 'Did you have good sleep?'

'Very good,' she said, trying not to think of the dreams and blushing slightly anyway. 'What can I do to help you?'

'No, no, you sit. I can do it.'

'You know I can't do that,' she chided softly. She stuck a mug under the coffee machine, pressed the button and waited, then added milk and went back to Carlotta, sipping the hot, fragrant brew gratefully. 'Oh, that's lovely. Right. What shall I do first?'

Carlotta gave in. 'We need to cut the meat, and the bread, and—'

'Just like yesterday?'

'*Si.*'

'So I'll do that, and you can make preparations for tonight. I know you have dinner to cook for the family as well as for the workers.'

Her brow creased, looking troubled, and Lydia could tell she was worried. Exhausted, more like. 'Look, let me do this, and maybe I can give you a hand with that, too?' she offered, but that was a step too far. Carlotta straightened her gnarled old spine and plodded to the fridge.

'I do it,' she said firmly, and so Lydia gave in and concentrated on preparing lunch for sixty people in the shortest possible time, so she could move on to cooking the pasta sauce for the evening shift with Maria. At least that way Carlotta would be free to concentrate on dinner.

Massimo found her in the kitchen at six, in the throes of draining gnocci for the workers, and she nearly dropped the pan. Crazy. Ridiculous, but the sight of him made her heart pound and she felt like a gangly teenager, awkward and confused because of the kiss.

'Are you in here again?' he asked, taking the other side of the huge pan and helping her tip it into the enormous strainer.

'Looks like me,' she said with a forced grin, but he just frowned and avoided her eyes, as if he, too, was feeling awkward and uncomfortable about the kiss.

'Did you speak to the hospital?' he asked, and she realised he would be glad to get rid of her. She'd been nothing but trouble for him, and she was unsettling the carefully constructed and safe status quo he'd created around them all.

'Yes. I'm fine to travel,' she said, although it wasn't quite true. They'd said they needed to examine her, and when she'd said she was too busy, they'd fussed a bit but what could they do? So she'd booked a flight. 'I've got a seat on a plane at three tomorrow afternoon from Pisa,' she told him, and he frowned again.

'Really? You didn't have to go so soon,' he said, confusing her even more.

'It's not soon. It'll be five days—that's what they said, and I've been under your feet long enough.'

And any longer, she realised, and things were going to happen between them. There was such a pull every time she was with him, and that kiss last night—

She thrust the big pot at him. 'Here, carry the *gnocci* outside for me. I'll bring the sauce.'

He followed her, set the food down for the workers and stood at her side, dishing up.

'So can I persuade you to join us for dinner?' he asked, but she shook her head.

'I've got nothing to wear,' she said, feeling safe because he couldn't argue with that, but she was wrong.

'You're about the same size as Serena. I'm sure she wouldn't mind if you borrowed something from her wardrobe. She always leaves something here. Carlotta will show you.'

'Carlotta's trying to prepare a meal for ten people this evening, Massimo. She doesn't have time to worry about clothes for me.'

'Then I'll take you,' he said, and the moment the serving was finishing, he hustled her back into the house before she could argue.

He was right. She and Serena were about the same size, something she already knew because she'd borrowed her costume to swim in, and she found a pair of black trousers that were the right length with her flat black pumps, and a pretty top that wasn't in the first flush of youth but was nice enough.

She didn't want to take anything too special, but she didn't think Serena would mind if she borrowed that one, and it was good enough, surely, for an interloper?

She went back to the kitchen, still in her jeans and T-shirt, and found Carlotta sitting at the table with her head on her arms, and Roberto beside her wringing his hands.

'Carlotta?'

'She is tired, *signorina*,' he explained worriedly. 'Signora Valtieri has many people for dinner, and my Carlotta…'

'I'll do it,' she said quickly, sitting down and taking Carlotta's hands in hers. 'Carlotta, tell me what you were going to cook them, and I'll do it.'

'But Massimo said…'

'Never mind what he said. I can cook and be there at the same time. Don't worry about me. We can make it easy. Just tell me what you're cooking, and Roberto can help me find things. We'll manage, and nobody need ever know.'

Her eyes filled with tears, and Lydia pulled a tissue out of a box and shoved it in her hand. 'Come on, stop that, it's all right. We've got cooking to do.'

Well, it wasn't her greatest meal ever, she thought as she sat with the others and Roberto waited on them, but it certainly didn't let Carlotta down, and from the compliments going back to the kitchen via Roberto, she knew Carlotta would be feeling much less worried.

As for her, in her borrowed top and trousers, she felt underdressed and overawed—not so much by the company as by the amazing dining room itself. Like her room and the kitchen, it opened to the terrace, but in the centre, with two pairs of double doors flung wide so they could hear the tweeting and twittering of the swallows swooping past the windows.

But it was the walls which stunned her. Murals again, like the ones in the cloistered walkway around the courtyard, but this time all over the ornate vaulted ceiling as well.

'Beautiful, isn't it?' Gio said quietly. 'I never

get tired of looking at this ceiling. And it's a good way to avoid my mother's attention.'

She nearly laughed at that. He was funny—very funny, very quick, very witty, very dry. A typical lawyer, she thought, used to brandishing his tongue in court like a rapier, slashing through the opposition. He would be formidable, she realised, and she didn't envy the woman who was so clearly still in love with him.

Anita was lovely, though. Strikingly beautiful, but warm and funny and kind, and Lydia wondered if she realised just how often Gio glanced at her when she'd looked away.

Elisa did, she was sure of it.

And then she met Massimo's eyes, and realised he was studying her thoughtfully.

'Excuse me, I have to go and do something in the kitchen,' she murmured. 'Carlotta very kindly let me experiment with the dessert, and I need to put the finishing touches to it.'

She bolted, running along the corridor and arriving in the kitchen just as Carlotta had put out the bowls.

'Roberto say you tell them I cook everything!' she said, wringing her hands and hugging her.

Lydia hugged her back. 'You did, really. I just helped you. You told me exactly what to do.'

'You *know* what to do. You such good *cuoca*—good cook. Look at this! So easy—so beautiful. *Bellisima*!'

She spread her hands wide, and Lydia looked. Five to a tray, there were ten individual gleaming white bowls, each containing glorious red and black frozen berries fogged with icy dew, and in the pan on the stove Roberto was gently heating the white chocolate sauce. Sickly sweet, immensely sticky and a perfect complement to the sharp berries, it was her favourite no-frills emergency pud, and she took the pan from Roberto, poured a swirl around the edge of each plate and then they grabbed a tray each and went back to the dining room.

'I hope you like it,' she said brightly. 'If not, please don't blame Carlotta, I made her let me try it!'

Elisa frowned slightly, but Massimo just gave her a level look, and as she set the plate down in front of him, he murmured, 'Liar,' softly, so only she could hear.

She flashed him a smile and went back to her

place, between Gio and Anita's father, and opposite Isabelle. 'So, tell me, what's it like living in Tuscany full-time?' she asked Isabelle, although she could see that she was blissfully contented and the answer was going to be biased.

'Wonderful,' Isabelle said, leaning her head against Luca's shoulder and smiling up at him. 'The family couldn't have been kinder.'

'That's not true. I tried to warn you off,' Gio said, and Luca laughed.

'You try and warn everybody off,' he said frankly, 'but luckily for me she didn't listen to you. Lydia, this dessert is amazing. Try it, *cara*.'

He held a spoonful up to Isabelle's lips, and Lydia felt a lump rise in her throat. Their love was so open and uncomplicated and genuine, so unlike the relationship she'd had with Russell. Isabelle and Luca were like Jen and Andy, unashamedly devoted to each other, and she wondered with a little ache what it must feel like to be the centre of someone's world, to be so clearly and deeply loved. *That* would be amazing.

She glanced across the table, and found Massimo watching her, his eyes thoughtful. He lifted his spoon to her in salute.

'Amazing, indeed.'

She blinked. He was talking about the dessert, not about love. Nothing to do with love, or with her, or him, or the two of them, or that kiss last night.

'Thank you,' she said, a little breathlessly, and turned her attention to the sickly, sticky white chocolate sauce. If she glued her tongue up enough with that, maybe it would keep it out of trouble.

'So how much of that was you, and how much was Carlotta?'

It was midnight, and everyone else had left or gone to bed. They were alone in the kitchen, putting away the last of the serving dishes that she'd just washed by hand, and Massimo was making her a cup of camomile tea.

'Honestly? I gave her a hand.'

'And the dessert?'

'Massimo, she was tired. She had all the ingredients for my quick fix, so I just improvised.'

'Hmm,' he said, but he left it at that, to her relief. She sensed he didn't believe her, but he had no proof, and Carlotta had been so distraught.

'Right, we're done here,' he said briskly. 'Let's go outside and sit and drink this.'

They went on her bench, outside her room, and sat in companionable silence drinking their tea. At least, it started out companionable, and then last night's kiss intruded, and she felt the tension creep in, making the air seem to fizz with the sparks that passed between them.

'You don't have to go tomorrow, you know,' he said, breaking the silence after it had stretched out into the hereafter.

'I do. I've bought a ticket.'

'I'll buy you another one. Wait a few more days.'

'Why? So I can finish falling for you? That's not a good idea, Massimo.'

He laughed softly, and she thought it was the saddest sound she'd ever heard. 'No. Probably not. I have nothing to offer you, Lydia. I wish I did.'

'I don't want anything.'

'That's not quite true. We both want something. It's just not wise.'

'Is it ever?'

'I don't know. Not for us, I don't think. We've both been hurt enough by the things that have happened, and I don't know about you but I'm not ready to try again. I have so many demands on me, so many calls on my time, so much *duty*.'

She put her cup down very carefully and turned to face him. 'We could just take tonight as it comes,' she said quietly, her heart in her mouth. 'No strings, just one night. No duty, no demands. Just a little time out from reality, for both of us.'

The silence was broken only by the beating of her heart, the roaring in her ears so loud that she could scarcely hear herself think. For an age he sat motionless, then he lifted a hand and touched her cheek.

'Why, *cara*? Why tonight?'

'Because it's our last chance?'

'Why me?'

'I don't know. It just seems right.'

Again he hesitated, then he took her hand and pressed it to his lips. 'Give me ten minutes. I need to check the children.'

She nodded, her mouth dry, and he brushed her lips with his and left her there, her fingers resting on the damp, tingling skin as if to hold the kiss in place.

Ten minutes, she thought. Ten minutes, and my life will change forever.

He didn't come back.

She gave up after half an hour, and went to bed

alone, humiliated and disappointed. How stupid, to proposition a man so far out of her league. He was probably still laughing at her in his room.

He wasn't. There was a soft knock on the door, and he walked in off the terrace. 'Lydia? I'm sorry I was so long. Are you still awake?'

She propped herself up on one elbow, trying to read his face, but his back was to the moonlight. 'Yes. What happened? I'd given up on you.'

'Antonino woke. He had a nightmare. He's all right now, but I didn't want to leave him till he was settled.'

He sat on the edge of the bed, his eyes shadowed in the darkness, and she reached for the bedside light. He caught her hand. 'No. Leave it off. Let's just have the moonlight.'

He opened the curtains wide, but closed the doors—for privacy? She didn't know, but she was grateful that he had because she felt suddenly vulnerable as he stripped off his clothes and turned back the covers, lying down beside her and taking her into his arms.

The shock of that first contact took their breath away, and he rested his head against hers and gave a shuddering sigh. 'Oh, Lydia, *cara*, you feel so good,' he murmured, and then after that she couldn't understand anything he said, because his voice deepened, the words slurred and incoherent. He was speaking Italian, she realised at last, his breath trembling over her body with every groaning sigh as his hands cupped and moulded her.

She arched against him, her body aching for him, a need like no need she'd ever felt swamping her common sense and turning her to jelly. She ran her hands over him, learning his contours, the feel of his skin like hot silk over the taut, corded muscles beneath, and then she tasted him, her tongue testing the salt of his skin, breathing in the warm musk and the lingering trace of cologne.

He seemed to be everywhere, his hands and mouth caressing every part of her, their legs tangling as his mouth returned to hers and he kissed her as if he'd die without her.

'Please,' she whispered, her voice shaking with need, and he paused, fumbling for something on the bedside table.

Taking care of her, she realised, something she'd utterly forgotten, but not him. He'd remembered, and made sure that she was safe with him.

No strings. No repercussions.

Then he reached for her, taking her into his arms, and as he moved over her she stopped thinking altogether and just *felt*.

He woke to the touch of her hand on his chest, lying lightly over his heart.

She was asleep, her head lying on his shoulder, her body silvered by the moonlight. He shifted carefully, and she sighed and let him go, so he could lever himself up and look down at her.

There was a dark stain over one hipbone. He hadn't noticed it last night, but now he did. A bruise, from her fall. And there was another, on her shoulder, and one on her thigh, high up on the side. He kissed them all, tracing the outline with his lips, kissing them better like the bruises of a child.

It worked, his brother Luca told him, because the caress released endorphins, feel-good hormones, and so you really could kiss someone better, but only surely if they were awake—

'Massimo?'

He turned his head and met her eyes. 'You're hurt all over.'

'I'm all right now.'

She smiled, reaching up and cradling his jaw in her hand, and he turned his face into her hand and kissed her palm, his tongue stroking softly over the sensitive skin.

'What time is it?'

He glanced at his watch and sighed. 'Two. Just after.'

Two. Her flight was in thirteen hours.

She swallowed hard and drew his face down to hers. 'Make love to me again,' she whispered.

How could he refuse? How could he walk away from her, even though it was madness?

Time out, she'd said, from reality. He needed that so badly, and he wasn't strong enough to resist.

Thirteen hours, he thought, and as he took her in his arms again, his heart squeezed in his chest.

Saying goodbye to the children and Carlotta and Roberto was hard. Saying goodbye to Massimo was agony.

He'd parked at the airport, in the short stay carpark, and they'd had lunch in the café, sitting outside under the trailing pergola. She positioned herself in the sun, but it didn't seem to be able to warm her, because she was cold inside, her heart aching.

'Thank you for everything you've done for me,' she said, trying hard not to cry, but it was difficult and she felt a tear escape and slither down her cheek.

'Oh, *bella*.' He sighed, and reaching out his hand, he brushed it gently away. 'No tears. Please, no tears.'

'Happy tears,' she lied. 'I've had a wonderful time.'

He nodded, but his eyes didn't look happy, and she was sure hers didn't. She tried to smile.

'Give my love to the children, and thank Francesca again for my Italian lessons.'

He smiled, his mouth turning down at the corners ruefully. 'They'll miss you. They had fun with you.'

'They'll forget me,' she reassured him. 'Children move on very quickly.'

But maybe not if they'd been hurt in the past, he thought, and wondered if this had been so safe after all, so without consequences, without repercussions.

Maybe not.

He left her at the departures gate, standing there with his arms round her while she hugged him tight. She let him go, looked up, her eyes sparkling with tears.

'Take care,' she said, and he nodded.

'You, too. Safe journey.'

And without waiting to see her go through the gate, he walked away, emotions raging through him.

Madness. He'd thought he could handle it, but—

He'd got her address from her, so he could send her a crate of wine and oil.

That was all, he told himself. Nothing more. He certainly wasn't going to contact her, or see her again—

He sucked in a breath, surprised by the sharp stab of loss. Ships in the night, he told himself more firmly. They'd had a good time but now it was over, she was gone and he could get on with his life.

How hard could it be?

# CHAPTER SIX

'WHY don't you just go and see her?'

Massimo looked up from the baby in his arms and forced himself to meet his brother's eyes.

'I don't know what you mean.'

'Of course you do. You've been like a grizzly bear for the last two weeks, and even your own children are avoiding you.'

He frowned. Were they? He hadn't noticed, he realised in horror, and winced at the wave of guilt. But…

'It's not a crime to want her, you know,' Luca said softly.

'It's not that simple.'

'Of course not. Love never is.'

His head jerked up again. 'Who's talking about love?' he snapped, and Luca just raised an eyebrow silently.

'I'm *not* in love with her.'

'If you say so.'

He opened his mouth to say, 'I do say so,' and shut it smartly. 'I've just been busy,' he said instead, making excuses. 'Carlotta's been ill, and I've been trying to juggle looking after the children in the evenings and getting them ready for school without neglecting all the work of the grape harvest.'

'But that's over now—at least the critical bit. And you're wrong, you know, Carlotta isn't ill, she's old and tired and she needs to stop working before she becomes ill.'

Massimo laughed out loud at that, startling his new nephew and making him cry. He shushed him automatically, soothing the fractious baby, and then looked up at Luca again. 'I'll let you tell her that.'

'I have done. She won't listen because she thinks she's indispensable and she doesn't want to let anybody down. And she's going to kill herself unless someone does something to stop her.'

And then it dawned on him. Just the germ of an idea, but if it worked…

He got to his feet, wanting to get started, now that the thought had germinated. He didn't know why he hadn't thought of it before, except he'd been deliberately putting it—her—out of his mind.

'I think I'll take a few days off,' he said casually. 'I could do with a break. I'll take the car and leave the children here. Mamma can look after them. It'll keep her off Gio's back for a while and they can play with little Annamaria while Isabelle rests.'

Luca took the baby from him and smiled knowingly.

'Give her my love.'

He frowned. 'Who? I don't know what you're talking about. This is a business trip. I have some trade samples to deliver.'

His brother laughed and shut the door behind him.

'Do you know anyone with a posh left-hand-drive Mercedes with a foreign number plate?'

Lydia's head jerked up. She did—but he wouldn't be here. There was no way he'd be here, and certainly not without warning—

'Tall, dark-haired, uber-sexy. Wow, in fact. Very, *very* wow!'

Her mouth dried, her heart thundering. No. Surely not—not when she was just getting over him—

'Let me see.'

She leant over Jen's shoulder and peeped through the doorway, and her heart, already racing, somersaulted in her chest. Over him? Not a chance. She'd been fooling herself for over two weeks, convincing herself she didn't care about him, it had just been a holiday romance, and one sight of him and all of it had come slamming back. She backed away, one hand on her heart, trying to stop it vaulting out through her ribs, the other over her mouth holding back the chaotic emotions that were threatening to erupt.

'It's him, isn't it? Your farmer guy. You never said he was that hot!'

No, she hadn't. She'd said very little about him because she'd been desperately trying to forget him and avoid the inevitable interrogation if she so much as hinted at a relationship. But—farmer? Try millionaire. More than that. Try serious landowner, old-money, from one of Italy's most well-known and respected families. Not a huge brand name, but big enough, she'd discovered when she'd checked on the internet in a moment of weakness and aching, pathetic need.

And try lover—just for one night, but the most magical, memorable and relived night of her life.

She looked down at herself and gave a tiny, desperate scream. She was cleaning tack—old, tatty tack from an even older, tattier pony who'd finally met his maker, and they were going to sell it. Not for much, but the saddle was good enough to raise a couple of hundred pounds towards Jen's wedding.

'He's looking around.'

So was she—for a way to escape from the tack room and back to the house without being seen, so she could clean up and at least look slightly less disreputable, but there was no other way out, and…

'He's seen me. He's coming over. Hi, there. Can I help?'

'I hope so. I'm looking for Lydia Fletcher.'

His voice made her heart thud even harder, and she backed into the shadows, clutching the filthy, soapy rag in a desperate fist.

'She's here,' Jen said, dumping her in it and flashing him her most charming smile. 'I'm her sister, Jen—and she's rather grubby, so she probably doesn't want you to see her like that, so why don't I take you over to the house and make you a cup of tea—'

'I don't mind if she's grubby. She's seen me looking worse, I'm sure.'

And before Jen could usher him away, he stepped past her into the tack room, sucking all the air out of it in that simple movement.

*'Ciao, bella,'* he said softly, a smile lurking in his eyes, and she felt all her resolve melt away to nothing.

*'Ciao,'* she echoed, and then toughened up. 'I didn't expect to see you again.'

She peered past him at Jen, hovering in the doorway. 'Why don't you go and put the kettle on?' she said firmly.

With a tiny, knowing smile, Jen took a step away, then mouthed, *'Be nice!'*

Nice? She had no intention of being anything *but* nice, but she also had absolutely no intention of being anything more accommodating. He'd been so clear about not wanting a relationship, and she'd thought she could handle their night together, thought she could walk away. Well, she wasn't letting him in again, because she'd never get over it a second time.

'You could have warned me you were coming,' she said when Jen had gone, her crutches scrunching in the gravel. 'And don't tell me you lost my phone number, because it was on the same piece of paper as my address, which you clearly have or you wouldn't be here.'

'I haven't lost it. I didn't want to give you the chance to avoid me.'

'You thought I would?'

'I thought you might want to, and I didn't want you to run away without hearing me out.' He looked around, studying the dusty room with the saddle racks screwed to the old beams, the saddle horse in the middle of the room with Bruno's saddle on it, half-cleaned, the hook dangling from the ceiling with his bridle and stirrup leathers hanging from it, still covered in mould and dust and old grease.

Just like her, really, smeared in soapy filth and not in any way dressed to impress.

'Evocative smell.' He fingered the saddle flap, rubbing his fingertips together and sniffing them. 'It takes me back. I had a friend with horses when

I was at boarding school over here, and I stayed with him sometimes. We used to have to clean the tack after we rode.'

He smiled, as if it was a good memory, and then he lifted his hand and touched a finger to her cheek. 'You've got dirt on your face.'

'I'm sure. And don't you dare spit on a tissue and rub it off.'

He chuckled, and shifting an old riding hat, he sat down on a rickety chair and crossed one foot over the other knee, his hands resting casually on his ankle as if he really didn't care how dirty the chair was.

'Well, don't let me stop you. You need to finish what you're doing—at least the saddle.'

She did. It was half-done, and she couldn't leave it like that or it would mark. She scrunched the rag in her fingers and nodded. 'If you don't mind.'

'Of course not. I didn't know you had a horse,' he added, after a slight pause.

'We don't—not any more.'

His eyes narrowed, and he leant forwards. 'Lydia?' he said softly, and she sniffed and turned away, reaching for the saddle soap.

'He died,' she said flatly. 'We don't need the

tack, so I'm going to sell it. It's a crime to let it rot out here when someone could be using it.'

'I'm sorry.'

'Don't be. He was ancient.'

'But you loved him.'

'Of course. That's what life's all about, isn't it? Loving things and losing them?' She put the rag down and turned back to him, her heart aching so badly that she was ready to howl her eyes out. 'Massimo, why are you here?'

'I promised you some olive oil and wine and balsamic vinegar.'

She blinked, and stared at him, dumbfounded. 'You drove all this way to deliver me *olive oil*? That's ridiculous. Why are you really here, in the middle of harvest? And what was that about not wanting me to run away before hearing you out?'

He smiled slowly—reluctantly. 'OK. I have a proposition for you. Finish the saddle, and I'll tell you.'

'Tell me now.'

'I'll tell you while you finish,' he compromised, so she picked up the rag again and reapplied it to the saddle, putting on rather more saddle soap than was necessary. He watched her, watched the fierce way she rubbed the leather, the pucker in her brow as she waited for him to speak.

'So?' she prompted, her patience running out.

'So—I think Carlotta is unwell. Luca says not, and he's the doctor. He says she's just old, and tired, and needs to stop before she kills herself.'

'I agree. She's been too old for years, probably, but I don't suppose she'll listen if you tell her that.'

'No. She won't. And the trouble is she won't allow anyone else in her kitchen.' He paused for a heartbeat. 'Anyone except *you*.'

She dropped the rag and spun round. 'Me!' she squeaked, and then swallowed hard. 'I—I don't understand! What have I got to do with anything?'

'We need someone to feed everybody for the harvest. After that, we'll need someone as a housekeeper. Carlotta won't give that up until she's dead, but we can get her local help, and draft in caterers for events like big dinner parties and so on. But for the harvest, we need someone she trusts who can cater for sixty people twice a day without getting in a flap—someone who knows what they're doing, who understands what's required and who's available.'

'I'm not available,' she said instantly, and he felt a sharp stab of disappointment.

'You have another job?'

She shook her head. 'No, not really, but I'm helping with the farm, and doing the odd bit of outside catering, a bit of relief work in the pub. Nothing much, but I'm trying to get my career back on track and I can't do that if I'm gallivanting about all over Tuscany, however much I want to help you out. I have to earn a living—'

'You haven't heard my proposition yet.'

She stared at him, trying to work out what he was getting at. What he was offering. She wasn't sure she wanted to know, because she had a feeling it would involve a lot of heartache, but—

'What proposition? I thought that was your proposition?'

'You come back with me, work for the harvest and I'll give your sister her wedding.'

She stared at him, confused. She couldn't have heard him right. 'I don't understand,' she said, finding her voice at last.

'It's not hard. The hotel was offering the ceremony, a reception for—what, fifty people?—a room for their wedding night, accommodation for the night before for the bridal party, a food and drink package—anything I've missed?'

She shook her head. 'Flowers, maybe?'

'OK. Well, we can offer all that. There's a chapel where they can marry, if they're Catholic, or they could have a blessing there and marry in the Town Hall, or whatever they wanted, and we'll give them a marquee with tables and chairs and a dance floor, and food and wine for the guests. And flowers. And if they don't want to stay in the guest wing of the villa, there's a lodge in the woods they can have the use of for their honeymoon.'

Her jaw dropped, and her eyes suddenly filled with tears. 'That's ridiculously generous! Why would you do this for them?'

'Because if I hadn't distracted you on the steps, you wouldn't have fallen, and your sister would have had her wedding.'

'No! Massimo, it wasn't your fault! I don't need your guilt as well as my own! This is not your problem.'

'Nevertheless, you would have won if you hadn't fallen, and yet when I took you back to my home that night you just waded in and helped Carlotta, even though you were hurt and disappointed. You didn't need to do that, but you saw she was struggling, and you put your own worries and injuries out of your mind and just quietly got on with it, even though you were much more sore than you let on.'

'What makes you say that?'

He smiled tenderly. 'I saw the bruises, cara. All over your body.'

She blushed furiously, stooping to pick the rag up off the floor, but it was covered in dust and she put it down again. The saddle was already soaped to death.

'And that dinner party—I know quite well that all of those dishes were yours. Carlotta doesn't cook like that, and yet you left an old woman her pride, and for that alone, I would give you this wedding for your sister.'

The tears spilled down her cheeks, and she scrubbed them away with the backs of her hands. Not a good idea, she realised instantly, when they were covered in soapy filth, but he was there in front of her, a tissue in his hand, wiping the tears away and the smears of dirt with them.

'Silly girl, there's no need to cry,' he tutted softly, and she pushed his hand away.

'Well, of course I'm crying, you idiot!' she sniffed, swallowing the tears. 'You're being ridiculously generous. But I can't possibly accept.'

'Why not? We need you—and that is real and genuine. I knew you'd refuse the wedding if I just offered it, but we really need help with the harvest, and it's the only way Carlotta will allow us to help her. If we do nothing, she'll work herself to death, but she'll be devastated if we bring in a total stranger to help out.'

'I was a total stranger,' she reminded him.

He gave that tender smile again, the one that had unravelled her before. 'Yes—but now you're a friend, and I'm asking you, as a friend, to help her.'

She swallowed. 'And in return you'll give Jen this amazing wedding?'

*'Si.'*

'And what about us?'

Something troubled flickered in his eyes for a second until the shutters came down. 'What about us?'

'We agreed it was just for one night.'

'Yes, we did. No strings. A little time out from reality.'

'And it stays that way?'

He inclined his head. '*Si*. It stays that way. It has to.'

Did it? She felt—what? Regret? Relief? A curious mixture of both, probably, although if she was honest she might have been hoping…

'Can I think about it?'

'Not for long. I have to return first thing tomorrow morning. I would like to take you with me.'

She nodded. 'Right. Um. I need to finish this—what are you *doing*?'

He'd taken off his jacket, slung it over the back of the chair and was rolling up his sleeves. 'Helping,' he said, and taking a clean rag from the pile, he buffed the saddle to a lovely, soft sheen. 'There. What else?'

It took them half an hour to clean the rest of Bruno's tack, and then she led him back to the house and showed him where he could wash his hands in the scullery sink.

'Don't mention any of this to Jen, not until I've

made up my mind,' she warned softly, and he nodded.

Her sister was in the kitchen, and she pointed her in the direction of the kettle and ran upstairs to shower. Ten minutes later, she was back down in the kitchen with her hair in soggy rats' tails and her face pink and shiny from the steam, but at least she was clean.

He glanced up at her and got to his feet with a smile. 'Better now?'

'Cleaner,' she said wryly. 'Is Jen looking after you?'

Jen was, she could see that. The teapot was on the table, and the packet of biscuits they'd been saving for visitors was largely demolished.

'She's been telling me all about you,' he said, making her panic, but Jen just grinned and helped herself to another biscuit.

'I've invited him to stay the night,' she said airily, dunking it in her tea while Lydia tried not to panic yet again.

'I haven't said yes,' he told her, his eyes laughing as he registered her reaction. 'There's a pub in the village with a sign saying they do rooms. I thought I might stay there.'

'You can't stay there. The pub's awful!' she said without thinking, and then could have kicked herself, because realistically there was nowhere else for miles.

She heard the door open, and the dogs came running in, tails wagging, straight up to him to check him out, and her mother was hard on their heels.

'Darling? Oh!'

She stopped in the doorway, searched his face as he straightened up from patting the dogs, and started to smile. 'Hello. I'm Maggie Fletcher, Lydia's mother, and I'm guessing from the number plate on your car you must be her Italian knight in shining armour.'

He laughed and held out his hand. 'Massimo Valtieri—but I'm not sure I'm any kind of a knight.'

'Well, you rescued my daughter, so I'm very grateful to you.'

'She hurt herself leaving my plane,' he pointed out, 'so really you should be throwing me out, not thanking me!'

'Well, I'll thank you anyway, for trying to get

her there in time to win the competition. I always said it was a crazy idea.'

'Me, too.' He smiled, and Lydia ground her teeth. The last thing she needed was him cosying up to her mother, but it got worse.

'I promised her some produce from the estate, and I thought, as I had a few days when I could get away, I'd deliver it in person. I'll bring it in, if I may?'

'Of course! How very kind of you.'

It wasn't kind. It was an excuse to bribe her into going back there to feed the troops by dangling a carrot in front of her that he knew perfectly well she'd be unable to resist. Two carrots, really, because as well as Jen's wedding, which was giving her the world's biggest guilt trip, there was the problem of the aging and devoted Carlotta, who'd become her friend.

'I'll help you,' she said hastily, following him out to the car so she could get him alone for a moment.

He was one step ahead of her, though, she realised, because as he popped the boot open, he turned to her, his face serious. 'Before you say anything, I'm not going to mention it to your family. This is entirely your decision, and if you decline, I won't say any more about it.'

Well, damn. He wasn't even going to *try* to talk her into it! Which, she thought with a surge of disappointment, could only mean that he really wasn't interested in picking up their relationship, and was going to leave it as it stood, as he'd said, with just that one night between them.

Not that she wanted him to do anything else. She really didn't want to get involved with another man, not after the hatchet job Russell had done on her self-esteem, and not when she was trying to resurrect her devastated career, but…

'Here. This is a case of our olive oils. There are three types, different varietals, and they're quite distinctive. Then this is a case of our wines—including a couple of bottles of vintage Brunello. You really need to save them for an important occasion, they're quite special. There's a nice *vinsanto* dessert wine in there, as well. And this is the *aceto balsamico* I promised you, from my cousin in Modena.'

While she was still standing there open-mouthed, he reached into a cool box and pulled out a leg of lamb and a whole Pecorino cheese.

'Something for your mother's larder,' he said with a smile, and without any warning she burst into tears.

'Hey,' he said softly, and wrapping his arms around her, he drew her up against his chest. He could feel the shudders running through her, and he cradled her against his heart and rocked her, shushing her gently. 'Lydia, please, *cara*, don't cry.'

'I'm not,' she lied, bunching her fists in his shirt and burrowing into his chest, and he chuckled and hugged her.

'I don't think that's quite true,' he murmured. 'Come on, it's just a few things.'

'It's nothing to do with the things,' she choked out. Her fist hit him squarely in the chest. 'I didn't think I'd ever see you again, and I was trying to move on, and then you just come back into my life and drop this bombshell on me about the wedding, and of all the times to choose, when I'm already…'

Realisation dawned, and he stroked her hair, gentling her. 'Oh, *cara*, I'm sorry. When did he die, the pony?'

She sniffed hard and tried to pull away, but he

wouldn't let her, he just held her tight, and after a moment she went still, unyielding but resigned. 'Last week,' she said, her voice clogged with tears. 'We found him dead in the field.'

'And you haven't cried,' he said.

She gave up fighting and let her head rest against his chest. 'No. But he was old.'

'We lost our dog last year. She was very, very old, and she'd been getting steadily worse. After she died, I didn't cry for weeks, and then one day it suddenly hit me and I disintegrated. Luca said he thought it was to do with Angelina. Sometimes grief is like that. We can't acknowledge it for the things that really hurt, and then something else comes along, and it's safe then to let go, to let out the hurt that you can't face.'

She lifted her head and looked up at him through her tears.

'But I don't hurt.'

'Don't you? Even after Russell treated you the way he did? For God's sake, Lydia, he was supposed to be your lover, and yet when he'd crippled your sister, his only reaction was anger that you'd left him and his business was suffering! What kind of a man is that? Of course you're hurting.'

She stared at him, hearing her feelings put into words somehow making sense of them all at last. She eased away from him, needing a little space, her emotions settling now.

'You know I can't say no, don't you? To your proposition?'

His mouth quirked slightly and he nodded slowly and let her go. 'Yes. I do know, and I realise it's unfair to ask this of you, but—I need help for Carlotta, and you need the wedding. This way, we both win.'

Or lose, depending on whether or not he could keep his heart intact, seeing her every day, working alongside her, knowing she'd be just there in the room beside his office, taunting him even in her sleep.

She met his eyes, her own troubled. 'I don't want an affair. I can't do it. One night was dangerous enough. I'm not ready, and I don't want to hurt your children.'

He nodded. 'I know. And I agree. If I wanted an affair, it would be with a woman my children would never meet, someone they wouldn't lose their hearts to. But I would like to be your friend,

Lydia. I don't know if that could work but I would like to try.'

No. It couldn't work. It was impossible, because she was already more than half in love with him, but—Jen needed her wedding, and she'd already had it snatched away from her once. This was another chance, equally as crazy, equally as dangerous, if not more so.

It was a chance she had to take.

'OK, I'll do it,' she said, without giving herself any further time to think, and his shoulders dropped slightly and he smiled.

'*Grazie, cara. Grazie mille.* And I know you aren't doing it for me, but for your sister and also for Carlotta, and for that, I thank you even more.'

He hugged her—just a gentle, affectionate hug between friends, or so he told himself as she slid her arms round him and hugged him back, but the feel of her in his arms, the soft pressure of her breasts, the smell of her shampoo and the warmth of her body against his all told him he was lying.

He was in this right up to his neck, and if he couldn't hold it together for the next two months—but he had to. There was no choice. Neither of them was ready for this.

He let her go, stepped back and dumped the lamb and the cheese in her arms. 'Let's go back in.'

'Talk to me about your dream wedding,' he said to Jen, after they'd taken all the things in from the car.

Her smile tugged his heartstrings. 'I don't dream about my wedding. The last time I did that, it turned into a nightmare for Lydia, so I'm keeping my feet firmly on the ground from now on, and we're going to do something very simple and quiet from here, and it'll be fine.'

'What if I was to offer you the *palazzo* as a venue?' he suggested, and Jen's jaw dropped.

'What?' she said, and then shook her head. 'I'm sorry, I don't understand.'

'The same deal as the hotel.'

She stared, looking from Lydia to Massimo and back again, and shook her head once more. 'I don't…'

'They need me,' Lydia explained. 'Carlotta's not well, and if I cook for the harvest season, you can have your wedding. I don't have another job yet, and it's good experience and an interesting place to work, so I thought it might be a good idea.'

'I've brought a DVD of my brother's wedding so you can see the setting. It might help you to decide.'

He handed it to her, and she handed it straight back.

'There's a catch,' she said, her voice strained. 'Lydia?'

'No catch. I work, you get the wedding.'

'But—that's so generous!'

'Nonsense. We'd have to pay a caterer to do the job, and it would cost easily as much.'

'But—Lydia, what about you? You were looking for another job, and you were talking about setting up an outside catering business. How can you do that if you're out of the country? No, I can't let you do it!'

'Tough, kid,' she said firmly, squashing her tears again. Heavens, she never cried, and this man was turning her into a fountain! 'I'm not doing it just for you, anyway. This is a job—a real job, believe me. And you know what I'm like. I'd love to know more about Italian food—real, proper country food—and this is my chance, so don't go getting all soppy on me, all right? My catering business will keep. Just say thank you and shut up.'

'Thank you and shut up,' she said meekly, and then burst into tears.

Lydia cooked the leg of lamb for supper and served it with rosemary roast potatoes and a redcurrant *jus*, and carrots and runner beans from the garden, and they all sat round at the battered old kitchen table with the dogs at their feet and opened one of the bottles of Brunello.

'It seems wrong, drinking it in here,' she said apologetically, 'but Andy's doing the accounts on the dining table at the moment and it's swamped.'

'It's not about the room, it's about the flavour. Just try it,' he said, watching her closely.

So she swirled it, sniffed it, rolled it round on her tongue and gave a glorious sigh. 'That is *the* most gorgeous wine I have ever tasted,' she told him, and he inclined his head and smiled.

'Thank you. We're very proud of it, and it's a perfect complement to the lamb. It's beautifully cooked. Well done.'

'Thank you. Thank you for trusting me with

it.' She smiled back, suddenly ridiculously happy, and then the men started to talk about farming, and Jen quizzed her about the *palazzo*, because she'd hardly said anything about it since she'd come home.

'It sounds amazing,' Jen said, wide-eyed. 'We'll have to look at that video.'

'You will. It's great. The frescoes are incredible, and the view is to die for, especially at night, when all you can see is the twinkling lights in the distance. It's just gorgeous, and really peaceful. I know it'll sound ridiculous, but it reminded me of home, in a way.'

'I don't think that's ridiculous,' Massimo said, cutting in with a smile. 'It's a home, that's all, just in a beautiful setting, and that's what you have here—a warm and loving family home in a peaceful setting. I'm flattered that you felt like that about mine.'

The conversation drifted on, with him telling them more about the farm, about the harvest and the soil and the weather patterns, and she could have sat there for hours just listening to his voice, but she had so much to do before they left in the morning, not least gathering together her clothes, so she left them all talking and went up to her room.

Bearing in mind she'd be flying back after the harvest was over, she tried to be sensible about the amount she took, but she'd need winter clothes as well as lighter garments, and walking boots so she could explore the countryside, and something respectable in case he sprang another dinner on her—

'You look lost.'

She looked up from her suitcase and sighed. 'I don't know what to take.'

'Your passport?'

'Got that,' she said, waggling it at him with a smile. 'It's clothes. I want enough, but not too much. I don't know what the weather will be like.'

'It can get cold. Bring warm things for later, but don't worry. You can buy anything you don't have.'

'I'm trying to stick to a sensible baggage allowance for when I come back.'

'Don't bother. I'll pay the excess. Just bring what you need.'

'What time are we leaving?'

'Seven.'

'Seven?' she squeaked, and he laughed.

'That's a concession. I would have left at five, or maybe six.'

'I'll be ready whenever you tell me. Have you been shown to your room?'

'*Si.* And the bathroom is opposite?'

'Yes. I'm sorry it doesn't have an *en suite* bathroom—'

'Lydia, stop apologising for your home,' he said gently. 'I'm perfectly capable of crossing a corridor. I'll see you at six for breakfast, OK?'

'OK,' she said, and for a heartbeat she wondered if he'd kiss her goodnight.

He didn't, and she spent a good half-hour trying to convince herself she was glad.

They set off in the morning shortly before seven, leaving Jen and Andy still slightly stunned and busy planning their wedding, and she settled back in the soft leather seat and wondered if she'd completely lost her mind.

'Which way are we going?' she asked as they headed down to Kent.

'The quickest route—northern France, across the Alps in Switzerland, past Lake Como and onto the A1 to Siena. We'll stay somewhere on the way. I don't want to drive through the Alps when I'm tired, the mountain roads can be a little tricky.'

Her heart thudded. They were staying somewhere overnight?

Well, of course they were, he couldn't possibly drive whatever distance it was from Suffolk to Tuscany in one day, but somehow she hadn't factored an overnight stop into her calculations, and the journey, which until now had seemed simple and straightforward, suddenly seemed fraught with the danger of derailing their best intentions.

## CHAPTER SEVEN

'LYDIA?'

She stirred, opened her eyes and blinked.

He'd pulled up in what looked like a motorway service area, and it was dark beyond the floodlit car park. She yawned hugely and wrapped her hand around the back of her neck, rolling her head to straighten out the kinks.

'Oh, ow. What time is it? I feel as if I've been asleep for hours!'

He gave her a wry, weary smile. 'You have. It's after nine, and I need to stop for the night before I join you and we have an accident.'

'Where are we?'

'A few miles into Switzerland? We're getting into the mountains and this place has rooms. It's a bit like factory farming, but it's clean and the beds are decent. I'd like to stop here if they have any vacancies.'

'And if they don't?'

He shrugged. 'We go on.'

But he must be exhausted. They'd only stopped twice, the last time at two for a late lunch. What if they only have one room? she thought, and her heart started to pound. How strong was her resolve? How strong was his?

She never found out. They had plenty of space, so he booked two rooms and carried her suitcase for her and put it down at the door. 'We should eat fairly soon, but I thought you might want to freshen up. Ten minutes?'

'Ten minutes is fine,' she said, and let herself into her lonely, barren motel room. It was clean and functional as he'd promised, just another generic hotel room like all the rest, and she wished that for once in her life she had the courage to go after the thing she really wanted.

Assuming the thing—the person—really wanted her, of course, and he'd made it clear he didn't.

She stared at herself in the bathroom mirror. What was she *thinking* about? She didn't want him! She wasn't ready for another relationship. Not really, not if she was being sensible. She wanted to get her career back on track, to refocus her life and remember where she was going and what she was doing. She certainly didn't need to get her heart broken by a sad and lonely workaholic ten years her senior, with three motherless children and a massively demanding business empire devouring all his time.

Even if he was the most fascinating and attractive man she'd ever met in her life, and one of the kindest and most thoughtful. He was hurting, too, still grieving for his wife, and in no way ready to commit to another relationship, no matter how deeply she might fall in love with him. He wouldn't hurt her intentionally, but letting herself get close to him—that was a recipe for disaster if nothing else was.

'Lydia?'

There was a knock at the bedroom door, and she turned off the bathroom light and opened it. Massimo was standing there in the corridor, in a fresh shirt and trousers, his hair still damp from the shower. He looked incredible.

'Are you ready for dinner?'

She conjured up a smile. 'Give me ten seconds.'

She picked up her bag, gave her lips a quick swipe of translucent colour as a concession to vanity and dragged a comb through her hair. And then, just out of defiance, she added a spritz of scent.

She might be travel weary, and she might not be about to get involved with him, but she still had her pride.

The dinner was adequate. Nothing more, nothing less.

He was tired, she was tired—and yet still they lingered, talking for an hour over their coffee. She asked about Isabelle and Luca's baby, and how the children were, and he asked her about Jen's progress and if she'd be off the crutches by the time of the wedding, whenever it would be.

They talked about his time at boarding school, and she told him about her own schooling, in a village just four miles from where she lived.

And then finally they both fell silent, and he looked at his watch in disbelief.

'It's late and tomorrow will be a hard drive,' he said. 'We should go to bed.'

The word *bed* reverberated in the air between them, and then she placed her napkin on the table and stood up a little abruptly. 'You're right. I'm sorry, you should have told me to shut up.'

He should. He should have cut it short and gone to bed, instead of sitting up with her and hanging on her every word. He paid the bill and escorted her back to her room, leaving a clear gap between them as he paused at her door.

Not because he wanted to, but because he didn't, and if he got any closer, he didn't trust himself to end it there.

*'Buonanotte, bella,'* he said softly. 'I'll wake you at five thirty.'

She nodded, and without looking back at him, she opened the door of her room, went in and closed it behind her. He stared at it for a second, gave a quiet, resigned laugh and let himself into his own room.

This was what he'd wanted, wasn't it? For her to keep her distance, to enable him to do the same?

So why did he suddenly feel so lonely?

It was like coming home.

This time, when she saw the fortress-like building standing proudly on the hilltop, she felt excitement and not trepidation, and when the children came tumbling down the steps to greet them, there was no look of horror, but shrieks of delight and hugs all round.

Antonino just wanted his father, but Francesca hugged her, and Lavinia hung on her arm and grinned wildly. 'Lydia!' she said, again and again, and then Carlotta appeared at the top of the steps and welcomed her—literally—with open arms.

'*Signorina*! You come back! Oh!'

She found herself engulfed in a warm and emotional hug, and when Carlotta let her go, her eyes were brimming. She blotted them, laughing at herself, and then taking Lydia by the hand, she led her through the courtyard to her old room.

This time there were flowers on the chest of drawers, and Roberto brought in her luggage and put it down and hugged her, too.

*'Grazie mille, signorina,'* he said, his voice choked. 'Thank you for coming back to help us.'

'Oh, Roberto, it's my pleasure. There's so much Carlotta can teach me, and I'm really looking forward to learning.'

'I teach,' she said, patting her hand. 'I teach you everything!'

She doubted it. Carlotta's knowledge of traditional dishes was a rich broth of inheritance, and it would take more than a few experiments to capture it, but it would still be fascinating.

They left her to settle in, and a moment later there was a tap at the French doors.

'The children and I are going for a swim. Want to join us?'

She was so tempted. It was still warm here, much warmer than in England, although she knew the temperature would drop once it was dark. The water in the pool would be warm and inviting, though, and it would be fun playing with the children, but she felt a shiver of danger, and not just from him.

'I don't think so. I'm a bit tired. I might rest for a little while.'

He nodded, smiled briefly and walked away, and she closed the door and shut the curtains, just to make the point.

The children were delightful, but they weren't why she was here, and neither was he. And the more often she reminded herself of that, the better, because she was in serious danger of forgetting.

She didn't have time to think about it.

The harvest season was in full swing, and from

first thing the following morning, she was busy. Carlotta still tried to do too much, but she just smiled and told her she was allowed to give orders and that was all, and after the first two days she seemed happy to do that.

She even started taking a siesta in the middle of the day, which gave Lydia time to make a lot of the preparations for the evening without prodding Carlotta's conscience.

And every evening, she dished up the food to the workers and joined them for their meal.

They seemed pleased to see her, and there was a bit of flirting and whistling and nudging, but she could deal with that. And then Massimo appeared at her side, and she heard a ripple of laughter and someone said something she'd heard a few times before when he was about. She'd also heard him say it to Francesca on occasions.

'What does *bella ragazza* mean?' she asked in a quiet moment as they were finishing their food, and he gave a slightly embarrassed laugh.

'Beautiful girl.'

She studied his face closely, unconvinced. 'Are you sure? Because they only say it when you're near me.'

He pulled a face. 'OK. It's usually used for a girlfriend.'

'They think I'm your *girlfriend*?' she squeaked, and he cleared his throat and pushed the food around his plate.

'Ignore them. They're just teasing us.'

Were they? Or could they see the pull between them? Because ignore it as hard as she liked, it wasn't going away, and it was getting stronger with every day that passed.

A few days later, while she was taking a breather out on the terrace before lunch, Isabelle appeared. She was pushing a pram, and she had a little girl in tow.

'Lydia, hi. I was hoping to find you. Mind if we join you?'

She stood up, pleased to see her again, and hugged her. 'Of course I don't mind. Congratulations! May I see?'

'Sure.'

She peered into the pram, and sighed. 'Oh, he's gorgeous. So, so gorgeous! All that dark hair!'

'Oh, yes, he's his daddy's boy. Sometimes I wonder where my genes went in all of this.' She laughed, and Lydia smiled and reached out to touch the sleeping baby's outstretched hand.

It clenched reflexively, closing on her fingertip, and she gave a soft sigh and swallowed hard.

He looked just like the picture of Antonino with his mother in the photo frame in the kitchen. Strong genes, indeed, she thought, and felt a sudden, shocking pang low down in her abdomen, a need so strong it was almost visceral.

She eased her finger away and straightened up. 'Can I get you a drink? And what about your little girl?'

'Annamaria, do you want a drink, darling?'

'Juice!'

'Please.'

'P'ees.'

'Good girl. I'd love a coffee, if you've got time? And anything juice-related with a big slosh of water would be great. We've got a feeder cup.'

They went into the kitchen, and she found some biscuits and took them out into the sun again with the drinks, and sat on the terrace under the pergola, shaded by the jasmine.

'Are you completely better now, after your fall?'

Isabelle asked her, and she laughed and brushed it aside.

'I'm fine. My ankle was the worst thing, really, but it's much better now. It still twinges if I'm careless, but it's OK. How about you? Heavens, you've had a baby, that's much worse!'

Isabelle laughed and shook her head. 'No. It was harder than when Annamaria was born, but really very straightforward, and you know Luca's an obstetrician?'

'Yes, I think so. I believe Massimo mentioned it. I know he's a doctor, he met us at the hospital when I had the fall and translated everything for me. So did he deliver him? What's he called, by the way?'

'Maximus—Max for short, after his uncle. Maximus and Massimo both mean the greatest, and my little Max was huge, so he really earned it. And yes, Luca did help deliver him, but at home with a midwife. Not like last time. He nearly missed Annamaria's birth, and I was at home on my own, so this time he kept a very close eye on me!'

'I'll bet. Wow. You're very brave having them at home.'

'No, I just have confidence in the process. I'm a midwife.'

'Is that how you met?'

She laughed. 'No. We met in Florence, in a café. We ended up together by a fluke, really.' She tipped her head on one side. 'So what's the story with you and Massimo?'

She felt herself colour and pretended to rearrange the biscuits. 'Oh, nothing, really. There is no story. He gave me a lift, I had an accident, he rescued me, and now I'm doing Carlotta's job so she doesn't kill herself.'

Isabelle didn't look convinced, but there was no way Lydia was going into details about her ridiculous crush or their one-night stand! But Luca's wife wasn't so easily put off. She let the subject drop for a moment, but only long enough to lift the now-crying baby from the pram and cradle him in her arms as she fed him.

Spellbound, Lydia watched the baby's tiny rosebud mouth fasten on his mother's nipple, saw the look of utter contentment on Isabelle's face, and felt a well of longing fill her chest.

'He's a good man, you know. A really decent

guy. He'd be worth the emotional investment, but only if you're serious. I'd hate to see him hurt.'

'He won't get hurt. We're not getting involved,' she said firmly. 'Yes, there's something there, but neither of us want it.'

Isabelle's eyes were searching, and Lydia felt as if she could see straight through her lies.

Lies? Were they?

Oh, yes. Because she did want it, even though it was crazy, even though she'd get horribly badly hurt. And she'd thought Russell had hurt her? He didn't even come close to what Massimo could do if she let him into her heart.

'He's not interested in an emotional investment,' she said, just in case there was any misunderstanding, but Isabelle just raised a brow slightly and smiled.

'No. He doesn't *think* he is, but actually he's ready to love again. He just hasn't realised it.'

'No, he isn't. We've talked about it—'

'Men don't talk. Not really. It's like pulling teeth. He's telling you what he thinks he ought to feel, not what he feels.'

She glanced up, at the same time as Lydia heard crunching on the gravel.

'Talk of the devil, here they are,' Isabelle said, smiling at her husband and his brother, and not wanting to get involved any deeper in this conversation, Lydia excused herself and went back to the kitchen.

Seconds later Massimo was in there behind her. 'I've come to tell you we've almost finished. The last of the vines are being stripped now and everyone's having the afternoon off.'

'So no lunch?'

He raised an eyebrow. 'I don't think you'll get away with that, but no evening meal, certainly. Not today. And tomorrow we're moving on to the chestnut woods. So tonight I'm taking you out for dinner, to thank you.'

'You don't need to do that. You're paying for my sister's wedding. That's thanks enough.'

He brushed it aside with a flick of his hand, and smiled. 'Humour me. I want to take you out to dinner. There's a place we eat from time to time—fantastic food, Toscana on a fork. The chef is Carlotta's great-nephew. I think you'll find it interesting. Our table's booked for eight.'

'What if I want an early night?'

'Do you?'

She gave in and smiled. 'No, not really. It sounds amazing. What's the dress code?'

'Clean. Nothing more. It's where the locals eat.'

'Your mother's a local,' she said drily, and he chuckled.

'My mother always dresses for the occasion. I'll wear jeans and a jacket, no tie. Does that help?'

She smiled. 'It does. Thank you. Help yourselves to coffee, I need to get on with lunch.'

Jeans and a jacket, no tie.

So what did that mean for her? Jeans? Best jeans with beaded embroidery on the back pockets and a pretty top?

Black trousers and a slinky top with a cardi over it?

A dress? How about a long skirt?

Clean. That was his first stipulation, so she decided to go with what was comfortable. And by eight, it would be cool, and they'd be coming back at about eleven, so definitely cooler.

Or maybe…

She'd just put the finishing touches to her makeup, not too much, just enough to make her feel she'd made the effort, when there was a tap on her door.

'Lydia? I'm ready to go when you are.'

She opened the door and scanned him. Jeans—good jeans, expensive jeans, with expensive Italian leather loafers and a handmade shirt, the leather jacket flung casually over his shoulder hanging from one finger.

He looked good enough to eat, and way up the scale of clean, so she was glad she'd changed her mind at the last minute and gone for her one decent dress. It wasn't expensive, but it hung like a dream to the asymmetric hem and made her feel amazing, and from the way he was scanning her, he wasn't disappointed.

'Will I do?' she asked, twirling slowly, and he said nothing for a second and then gave a soft huff of laughter.

'Oh, yes. I think so.'

His eyes were still trailing over her, lingering on the soft swell of her breasts, the curve of her hip, the hint of a thigh—

He pulled himself together and jerked his eyes back up to meet hers. 'You look lovely,' he said, trying not to embarrass himself or her. 'Are you ready to go?'

'I just need a wrap for later.' She picked up a pretty pashmina the same colour as her eyes, and her bag, and shut the door behind her. 'Right, then. Let's go get Toscana on a fork!'

It was a simple little building on one side of a square in the nearby town.

From the outside it looked utterly unpretentious, and it was no different inside. Scrubbed tables, plain wooden chairs, simple décor. But the smell was amazing, and the place was packed.

'Massimo, *ciao*!'

He shook hands with a couple on the way in, introduced her as a friend from England, and ushered her past them to the table he'd reserved by the window.

'Is it always this busy?'

His lips twitched in a smile. 'No. Sometimes it's full.'

She looked around and laughed. 'And these are all locals?'

'Mostly. Some will be tourists, people who've bothered to ask where they should eat.'

She looked around again. 'Is there a menu?'

'No. He writes it on a board—it's up there. Tonight it's a casserole of wild boar with plums in a red wine reduction.'

'And that's it?'

'No. He cooks a few things every night—you can choose from the board, but the first thing up is always his dish of the day, and it's always worth having.'

She nodded. 'Sounds great.'

He ordered a half-carafe of house wine to go with it—again, the wine was always chosen to go with the meal and so was the one to go for, he explained—and then they settled back to wait.

'So—are you pleased with the harvest?' she asked to fill the silence, and he nodded.

'*Si*. The grapes have been exceptional this year, it should be an excellent vintage. We need that. Last year was not so good, but the olives were better, so we made up for it.'

'And how are the olives this year?'

'Good so far. It depends on the weather. We need a long, mild autumn to let them swell and ripen before the first frosts. We need to harvest early enough to get the sharp tang from the olives, but not so early that it's bitter, or so late that it's sweet and just like any other olive oil.'

She smiled. 'That's farming for you. Juggling the weather all the time.'

'*Si.* It can be a disaster or a triumph, and you never know. We're big enough to weather it, so we're fortunate.'

'We're not. We had a dreadful year about three years ago, and I thought we'd go under, but then the next year we had bumper crops. It's living on a knife edge that's so hard.'

'Always. Always the knife edge.'

Her eyes met his, and the smile that was hovering there was driven out by an intensity that stole her breath away. 'You look beautiful tonight, *cara,*' he said softly, reaching out to touch her hand where it lay on the table top beside her glass.

She withdrew it, met his eyes again warily. 'I thought we weren't going to do this?'

'We're not doing anything. It was a simple compliment. I would say the same to my sister.'

'No, you wouldn't. Not like that.' She picked up her glass of water and drained the last inch, her mouth suddenly dry. 'At least, I hope not.'

His mouth flicked up briefly at the corners. 'Perhaps not quite like that.'

He leant back as the waiter appeared, setting down bread and olive oil and balsamic vinegar, and she tore off a piece of bread and dunked it, then frowned thoughtfully as the taste exploded on her tongue. 'Is this yours?'

He smiled. 'Yes. And the *balsamico* is from my cousin.'

'And the wild boar?'

'I have no idea. If it's from our estate, I don't know about it. The hunting season doesn't start until November.'

She smiled, and the tension eased a little, but it was still there, simmering under the surface, the compliment hovering at the fringes of her consciousness the whole evening. It didn't spoil the meal. Rather, it heightened the sensations of taste and smell and texture, as if somehow his words had brought her alive again and set her free.

'This casserole is amazing,' she said after the first mouthful. 'I want the recipe.'

He laughed at that. 'He won't give it to you. Women offer to sleep with him, but he never reveals his secrets.'

'Does he sleep with them anyway?'

He chuckled again. 'I doubt it. His wife would skin him alive.'

'Good for her. She needs to keep him. He's a treasure. And I've never been that desperate for a recipe.'

'I'm glad to hear it.' He was. He didn't even want to think about her sleeping with anybody else, even if she wasn't sleeping with him. And she wasn't.

She really, really wasn't. He wasn't going to do that again, it was emotional suicide. It had taken him over a week before he could sleep without waking aroused and frustrated in a tangle of sheets, aching for her.

He returned his attention to the casserole, mopping up the last of the sauce with a piece of bread until finally the plate was clean and he had no choice but to sit back and look up and meet her eyes.

'That was amazing,' she said. 'Thank you so much.'

'Dessert?'

She laughed a little weakly. 'I couldn't fit it in. Coffee, though—I could manage coffee.'

He ordered coffee, and they lingered over it, almost as if they daren't leave the safety of the little *trattoria* for fear of what they might do. But then they ran out of words, out of stalling tactics, and their eyes met and held.

'Shall we go?'

She nodded, getting to her feet even though she knew what was going to happen, knew how dangerous it was to her to leave with him and go back to her room—because they would end up there, she was sure of it, just as they had before, and all their good intentions would fall at the first hurdle…

# CHAPTER EIGHT

THEY didn't speak on the way back to the *palazzo*.

She sat beside him, her heart in her mouth, the air between them so thick with tension she could scarcely breathe. They didn't touch. All the way to her bedroom door, there was a space between them, as if they realised that the slightest contact would be all it took to send them up in flames.

Even when he shut the door behind them, they still hesitated, their eyes locked. And then he closed his eyes and murmured something in Italian. It could have been a prayer, or a curse, or just a 'what the hell am I doing?'

She could understand that. She was doing it herself, but she was beyond altering the course of events. She'd been beyond it, she realised, the moment he'd walked into the tack room at home and smiled at her.

He opened his eyes again, and there was resignation in them, and a longing that made her want to weep. He lifted his hand and touched her cheek, just lightly, but it was enough.

She turned her face into his hand, pressing her lips to his palm, and with a ragged groan he reeled her in, his mouth finding hers in a kiss that should have felt savage but was oddly tender for all its desperation.

His jacket hit the floor, then his shirt, stripped off over his head, and he spun her round, searching for the zip on her dress and following its progress with his lips, scorching a trail of fire down her spine. It fell away, and he unclipped her bra and turned her back to face him, easing it away and sighing softly as he lowered his head to her breasts.

She felt the rasp of his stubble against the sensitised skin, the heat of his mouth closing over one nipple, then the cold as he blew lightly against the dampened flesh.

She clung to his shoulders, her legs buckling, and he scooped her up and dropped her in the middle of the bed, stripping off the rest of his clothes before coming down beside her, skin to skin, heart to heart.

There was no foreplay. She would have died if he'd made her wait another second for him. Incoherent with need, she reached for him, and he was there, his eyes locking with hers as he claimed her with one long, slow thrust.

His head fell against hers, his eyes fluttering closed, a deep groan echoing in her ear. Her hands were on him, sliding down his back, feeling the powerful muscles bunching with restraint, the taut buttocks, the solid thighs bracing him as he thrust into her, his restraint gone now, the desperation overwhelming them, driving them both over the edge into frenzy.

She heard a muffled groan, felt his lips against her throat, his skin like hot, wet silk under her hands as his hard body shuddered against hers. For a long time he didn't move, but then, his chest heaving, he lifted his head to stare down into her eyes.

'Oh, *cara*,' he murmured roughly, and then gathering her against his heart he rolled to his side and collapsed against the pillows, and they lay there, limbs entangled, her head on his chest, and waited for the shockwaves to die away.

* * *

'I thought we weren't going to do that.'

He glanced down at her, and his eyes were filled with regret and despair. 'It looks like we were both wrong.'

His eyes closed, as if he couldn't bear to look at her, and easing away from her embrace he rolled away and sat up on the edge of the bed, elbows braced on his knees, dropping his head into his hands for a moment. Then he raked his fingers through his hair and stood up, pulling on his clothes.

'I have to check the children,' he said gruffly.

'We need to talk.'

'Yes, but not now. Please, *cara*. Not now.'

He couldn't talk to her now. He had to get out of there, before he did something stupid like make love to her again.

Make love? Who was he kidding? He'd slaked himself on her, with no finesse, no delicacy, no patience. And he'd promised her—promised himself, but promised *her*—that this wouldn't happen again.

Shaking his head in disgust, he pushed his feet into his shoes, slung his jacket over his shoulder and then steeled himself to look at her.

She was still lying there, curled on her side on top of the tangled bedding, her eyes wide with hurt and confusion.

'Massimo?'

'Later. Tomorrow, perhaps. I have to go. If Antonino wakes—'

She nodded, her eyes closing softly as she bit her lip. Holding back the tears?

He was despicable. All he ever did was make this woman cry.

He let himself out without another word, and went through to his part of the house, up the stairs to the children to check that they were all in bed and sleeping peacefully.

They were. Antonino had kicked off the covers, and he eased them back over his son and dropped a kiss lightly on his forehead. He mumbled in his sleep and rolled over, and he went out, leaving the door open, and checked the girls.

They were both asleep, Francesca's door closed, Lavinia's open and her nightlight on.

He closed the landing door that led to his parents' quarters, as he always did when he was in the house, and then he made his way back down to the kitchen and poured himself a glass of wine.

Why? Why on earth had he been so stupid? After all his lectures to himself, how could he have been so foolish, so weak, so self-centred?

He'd have to talk to her, he realised, but he had no idea what he would say. He'd promised her—promised! And yet again he'd failed.

He propped his elbows on the table and rested his face in his hands. Of all the idiotic things—

'Massimo?'

Her voice stroked him like a lover's touch, and he lifted his head and met her eyes.

'What are you doing here?' he asked, his voice rough.

'I came to get a drink,' she said uncertainly.

He shrugged. 'Go ahead, get it.'

She stayed there, her eyes searching his face. 'Oh, Massimo, don't beat yourself up. We were deluded if we thought this wouldn't happen. It was so obvious it was going to and I can't believe we didn't realise. What we need to work out is what happens now.'

He gave a short, despairing laugh and pushed back his chair. 'Nothing, but I have no idea how to achieve that. All I know that whenever I'm with you, I want you, and I can't just have what I want.

I'm not a tiny child, I understand the word no, I just can't seem to use it to myself. Wine?'

She shook her head. 'Tea. I'll make it.'

He watched her as she took out a mug from the cupboard, put a teabag in it, poured on boiling water, her movements automatic. She was wearing a silky, figure-hugging dressing gown belted round her waist, and he'd bet his life she had those tiny little pyjamas on underneath.

'Just tell me this,' she said at last, turning to face him. 'Is there any reason why we can't have an affair? Just—discreetly?'

'Here? In this house? Are you crazy? I have children here and they have enough to contend with without waking in the night from a bad dream and finding I'm not here because I'm doing something stupid and irresponsible for my own gratification.'

She sat down opposite him, cradling the tea in her hands and ignoring his stream of self-hatred. 'So what do you normally do?'

Normally? *Normally?* he thought.

'Normally, I don't have affairs,' he said flatly. 'I suppose, if I did, it would be elsewhere.' He shrugged. 'Arranged meetings—afternoon liaisons when the children are at school, lunchtimes, coffee.'

'And does it work?'

He laughed a little desperately. 'I have no idea. I've never tried.'

She stared at him in astonishment. 'What? In five years, you've never had an affair?'

'Not what you could call an affair, no. I've had the odd liaison, but nothing you could in any way call a relationship.' He sighed shortly, swirled his wine, put it down again.

'You have to see it from my point of view. I have obligations, responsibilities. I would have to be very, very circumspect in any relationship with a woman.'

'Because of the children.'

'Mostly, but because of all sorts of things. Because of my duties and responsibilities, the position I hold within the family, the business—any woman I was to become involved with would have to meet a very stringent set of criteria.'

'Not money-grabbing, not lying, not cheating, not looking for a meal ticket or an easy family or status in the community.'

'Exactly. And it's more trouble than it's worth. I

don't need it. I can live without the hassle. But it's more than that. If I make a mistake, many people could suffer. And besides, I don't have the time to invest in a relationship, not to do it justice. And nor do you, not if you're going to reinvent yourself and relaunch your career.'

*He'd be worth the emotional investment, but only if you're serious.*

*Oh, Isabelle, you're so right,* she thought. But was she serious? Serious enough? Could she afford to dedicate the emotional energy needed, to a man who was so clearly focused on his family life and business that women weren't considered necessary?

If she felt she stood the slightest chance, then yes, she realised, she could be very, very serious indeed about this man. But he wasn't ever going to be serious about her. Not serious enough to let her into all parts of his life, and there was no way she'd pass his stringent criteria test.

No job, for a start. No independent wealth—no wealth of any sort. And besides, he was right, she needed to get her career back on track. It had been going so well…

'So what happens now? We can't have an affair here, because of the children, and yet we can't seem to stick to that. So what do we do? Because doing nothing doesn't seem to work for us, Massimo. We need a plan.'

He gave a wry laugh and met her eyes again, his deadly serious. 'I have no idea, *cara*. I just know I can't be around you.'

'So we avoid each other?'

'We're both busy. It shouldn't be so hard.'

They were busy, he was right, but she felt a pang of loss even though she knew it made sense.

'OK. I'll keep out of your way if you keep out of mine.'

He inclined his head, then looked up as she got to her feet.

'You haven't finished your tea.'

'I'll take it with me,' she said, and left him sitting there wondering why he felt as if he'd just lost the most precious thing in the world, and yet didn't quite know what it was.

Nice theory, she thought later, when her emotions had returned to a more even keel. It just didn't have a hope of working in practice.

How could they possibly avoid each other in such an intimate setting?

Answer—they couldn't. He was in and out of the kitchen all the time with the children, and she was in and out of his workspace twice a day at least with food for the team of workers.

They were gathering chestnuts this week, in the *castagneti*, the chestnut woods on the higher slopes at the southern end of the estate. Carlotta told her all about it, showed her the book of chestnut recipes she'd gathered, many handed down from her mother or her grandmother, and she wanted to experiment.

So she asked Massimo one lunchtime if she could have some for cooking.

'Sure,' he said briskly. 'Help yourself. Someone will give you a basket.'

She shouldn't have been hurt. It was silly. She knew why he was doing it, why he hadn't met her eyes for more than a fleeting second, because in that fleeting second she'd seen something in his eyes that she recognised.

A curious mixture of pain and longing, held firmly in check.

She knew all about that.

She gathered her own chestnuts, joining the workforce and taking good-natured and teasing advice, most of which she didn't understand, because her Italian lessons with Francesca hadn't got that far yet—and in any case, she was very conscious of not getting too close to his children, for fear of them forming an attachment to her that would only hurt them when she went home again, so she hadn't encouraged it.

But she understood the gist. Sign language was pretty universal, and she learned how to split open the cases without hurting her fingers and remove the chestnuts—huge chestnuts, *marrone*, apparently—and that night after she'd given them all their evening meal, she went into the kitchen to experiment.

And he was there, sitting at the kitchen table with a laptop and a glass of wine.

'Oh,' she said, and stood there stupidly for a moment.

'Problem?'

'I was going to try cooking some of the chestnuts.'

His eyes met hers, and he shut the laptop and stood up. 'It's fine. I'll get out of your way.'

She looked guarded, he thought, her sunny smile and open friendliness wiped away by his lack of control and this overwhelming need that stalked him hour by hour. It saddened him. Greatly.

'You don't have to go.'

'I do,' he said wearily. 'I can't be around you, *cara*. It's too difficult. I thought I could do this, but I can't. The only way is to keep my distance.'

'But you can't. We're falling over each other all the time.'

'There's no choice.'

There was, she thought. They could just go with the flow, make sure they were discreet, keep it under control, but he didn't seem to think they could do that successfully, and he'd left the kitchen anyway.

She sat down at the table, in the same chair, feeling the warmth from his body lingering in the wood, and opened Carlotta's recipe book. Pointless. It was in Italian, and she didn't understand a word.

Frustration getting the better of her, she dropped her head into her hands and growled softly.

'Lydia, don't.'

'Don't what? I thought you'd gone,' she said, lifting her head.

'I had.' He sat down opposite her and took her hand in his, the contact curiously disturbing and yet soothing all at once.

'This is driving me crazy,' he admitted softly.

'Me, too. There must be another way. We can't avoid each other successfully, so why don't we just work alongside each other and take what comes? We know it's not long-term, we know you're not looking for commitment and I'm not ready to risk it again, and I have to go back and try and re-launch my career in some direction.'

He let go of her hand and sat back. 'Any ideas for that?' he said, not running away again as she'd expected, but staying to have a sensible conversation, and she let herself relax and began to talk, outlining her plans, such as they were.

'I've been thinking more and more about outside catering, using produce from my parents' farm. There are plenty of people with money living in the nearby villages, lots of second homes with people coming up for the weekend and bringing friends. I'm sure there would be openings, I just have to be there to find them.'

'It could be a bit seasonal.'

'Probably. Easter, summer and winter—well, Christmas and New Year, mostly. There's always lots of demand around Christmas, and I need to be back by then. Will the olive harvest be over?'

'Almost certainly. If it's not, we can manage if you need to return.' He stood up and put the kettle on. 'I was thinking we should invite your sister and her fiancé over to meet Anita so she can start the ball rolling.'

'Anita?'

'*Si*. They'll need a wedding planner.'

'They can't afford a wedding planner!'

'It's part of the package. I'm not planning it, I simply don't have the time or the expertise, and Jen can't plan a wedding in a strange place from a distance of two thousand kilometres, so we need Anita.'

'I could do it. I'm here.'

'But do you have the necessary local contacts? No. And besides, you're already busy.'

'Can I do the catering?'

He smiled tolerantly. 'Really? Wouldn't you rather enjoy your sister's wedding?'

'No. I'd rather cut down the cost of it to you. I feel guilty enough—'

'Don't feel guilty.'

'But I do. I know quite well what cooks get paid, and it doesn't stack up to the cost of a wedding in just three months!'

He smiled again. 'We pay our staff well.'

She snorted rudely, and found a mug of tea put down in front of her.

'Don't argue with me, *cara*,' he said quietly. 'Just ask your sister when she could come over, and arrange the flights and check that Anita is free to see them.'

'Only if you'll let me do the catering.'

He rolled his eyes and laughed softly. 'OK, you can do the catering, but Anita will give you menu options.'

'No. I want to do the menus.'

'Why are you so stubborn?'

'Because it's my job!'

'To be stubborn?'

'To plan menus. And don't be obtuse.'

His mouth twitched and he sat down opposite her again, swirling his wine in the glass. 'I thought you were going to cook chestnuts?'

'I can't read the recipe book. My Italian is extremely limited so it's a non-starter.'

He took it from her, opened it and frowned. 'Ah. Well, some of it is in a local dialect anyway.'

'Can you translate?'

'Of course. But you'd need to know more than just classic Italian to understand it. Which recipe did you want to try?'

She raised an eyebrow. 'Well, how do I know? I don't know what they are.'

'I'll read them to you.'

'You know what? I'll do it in the morning, with Carlotta. She'll be able to tell me which are her favourites.'

'I can tell you that. She feeds them to us regularly. She does an amazing mousse for dessert, and stuffing for roast boar which is incredible. You should get her to teach you those if nothing else. Anyway, tomorrow won't work. There's a fair in the town.'

'Carlotta said there was a day off, but nobody told me why.'

'To celebrate the end of *La Vendemmia*. They hold one every year. Then in a few weeks there's the chestnut fair, and then after *La Raccolta*, the olive harvest, there's another one. It's a sort of harvest festival gone mad. You ought to go tomorrow, it's a good day out.'

'Will you be there?'

He nodded. 'All of us will be there.'

'I thought we were avoiding each other?'

He didn't smile, as she'd expected. Instead he frowned, his eyes troubled. 'We are. I'll be with my children. Roberto and Carlotta will be going. I'm sure they'll give you a lift.'

And then, as if she'd reminded him of their unsatisfactory arrangement, he stood up. 'I'm going to do some work. I'll see you tomorrow.'

She did see him, but only because she kept falling over him.

Why was it, she thought, that if you lost someone in a crowd of that size you'd never be able to find them again, and yet every time she turned round, he was there?

Sometimes he didn't see her. Equally, probably, there were times when she didn't see him. But there were times when their eyes met, and held. And then he'd turn away.

Well, this time she turned away first, and made

her way through the crowd in the opposite direction.

And bumped into Anita.

'Lydia! I was hoping I'd see you. Come, let's find a quiet corner for a coffee and a chat. We have a wedding to plan!'

She looked around at the jostling crowd and laughed. 'A quiet corner?'

'There must be one. Come, I know a café bar on a side street. We'll go there.'

They had to sit outside, but the sunshine was lovely and it was relatively quiet away from the hubbub and festival atmosphere of the colourful event.

'So—this wedding. Massimo tells me your sister's coming over soon to talk about it. Do you know what she wants?'

Lydia shrugged, still uncomfortable about him spending money on Anita's services. 'The hotel was offering a fairly basic package,' she began, and Anita gave a soft laugh.

'I know the hotel. It would have been basic, and they would have talked it up to add in all sorts of things you don't really need.'

'Well, they wouldn't, because she hasn't got any money, which is why I'm working here now.'

Anita raised an eyebrow slightly. 'Is that the only reason?' she asked softly. 'Because I know these Valtieri men. They're notoriously addictive.'

Poor Anita. Lydia could see the ache in her eyes, knew that she could understand. Maybe, for that reason, she let down her guard.

'No. It's not the only reason,' she admitted quietly. 'Maybe, subconsciously, it gave me an excuse to spend time with him, but trust me, it's not going to come to anything.'

'Don't be too sure. He's lonely, and he's a good man. He can be a bit of a recluse—he shuts himself away and works rather than deal with his emotions, but he's not alone in that. It's a family habit, I'm afraid.'

She shook her head. 'I *am* sure nothing will come of it. We've talked about it,' she said, echoing her conversation with Isabelle and wondering if both women could be wrong or if it was just that they were fond of him and wanted him to be happy.

'He needs someone like you,' Anita said, 'someone honest and straightforward who isn't afraid of hard work and understands the pressures and demands of an agricultural lifestyle. He said your family are lovely, and he felt at home there with them. He said they were refreshingly unpretentious.'

She laughed at that. 'We've got nothing to be pretentious about,' she pointed out, but Anita just smiled.

'You have to understand where he's coming from. He has women after him all the time. He's a very, very good catch, and Gio is worried that some money-seeking little tart will get her claws into him.'

'Not a chance. He's much too wary for that, believe me. He has strict criteria. Anyway, I thought we were talking about the wedding?'

Anita smiled wryly and let it go, but Lydia had a feeling that the subject was by no means closed…

'What are you doing?'

A pair of feet appeared in her line of sight, slender feet clad in beautiful, soft leather pumps. She straightened up on her knees and looked up at his mother, standing above her on the beautiful frescoed staircase.

'I'm helping Carlotta.'

'It's not your job to clean. She has a maid for that.'

'But the maid's sick, so I thought I'd help her.'

Elisa frowned. 'I didn't know that. Why didn't Carlotta tell me?'

'Because she doesn't?' she suggested gently. 'She just gets on with it.'

'And so do you,' his mother said softly, coming down to her level. 'Dear girl, you shouldn't be doing this. It's not part of your job.'

'I don't have a job, Signora Valtieri. I have a bargain with your son. I help out, my sister gets her wedding, which is incredibly generous, so if there's some way I can help, I just do it.'

'You do, don't you, without any fuss? You are a quite remarkable girl. It's a shame you have to leave.'

'I don't think he thinks so.'

'My son doesn't know what's good for him.'

'And you do?'

'Yes, I do, and I believe you could be.'

She stared at Elisa, stunned. 'But—I'm just a chef. A nobody.'

'No, you are not a nobody, Lydia, and we're just farmers like your people.'

'No.' She laughed at that and swept an arm around her to underline her point. 'No, you're not just farmers, *signora*. My family are just farmers. You own half of Tuscany and a *palazzo*, with incredibly valuable frescoes on the walls painted by Old Masters. There is a monumental difference.'

'I think not—and please stop calling me *signora*. My name, as you well know, is Elisa. Come. Let's go and get some coffee and have a chat.'

She shook her head. 'I can't. I have work to do—lunch to prepare for everyone in a minute. I was just giving the stairs a quick sweep.'

'So stop now, and come, just for a minute. Please? I want to ask you something.'

It was a request, but from his mother it was something on the lines of an invitation to Buckingham Palace. You didn't argue. You just went.

So she went, leaving the ornate and exquisitely painted staircase hall and following her into the smaller kitchen which served their wing of the house.

'How do you take your coffee? Would you like a cappuccino?'

'That would be lovely. Thank you.'

Bone china cups, she thought, and a plate with little Amaretti biscuits. Whatever this was about, it was not going to be a quick anything, she realised.

'So,' Elisa said, setting the tray down at a low table between two beautiful sofas in the formal *salon* overlooking the terrace. 'I have a favour to ask you. My son tells me you're contemplating starting a catering business. I would like to commission you.'

Lydia felt her jaw drop. 'Commission?' she echoed faintly. 'For what?'

'I'm having a meeting of my book group. We get together every month over dinner and discuss a book we've read, and this time it's my turn. I would like you to provide the meal for us. There will be twenty people, and we will need five courses.'

She felt her jaw sag again. 'When?'

'Wednesday next week. The chestnuts should be largely harvested by then, and the olive harvest won't have started yet. So—will you do it?'

'Is there a budget?'

Elisa shrugged. 'Whatever it takes to do the job.'

Was it a test? To see if she was good enough? Or a way to make her feel valued and important enough to be a contender for her son? Or was it simply that she needed a meal provided and Carlotta was too unwell?

It didn't matter. Whatever the reason, she couldn't refuse. She looked into Elisa's eyes.

'Yes. Yes, I'll do it,' she said. 'Just so long as you'll give me a reference.'

Elisa put her cup down with a satisfied smile. 'Of course.'

## CHAPTER NINE

THE book club dinner seemed to be going well.

She was using her usual kitchen—the room which historically had always been the main kitchen in the house, although it was now used by Massimo and his children, and for preparing the harvest meals.

She needed the space. Twenty people were quite hard to cater for if the menu was extravagant, and she'd drafted in help in the form of Maria, the girl who'd been helping her with the meals all along.

The *antipasti* to start had been a selection of tiny canapés, all bite-sized but labour intensive. Massimo had dropped in and tasted them, and she'd had to send him away before he'd eaten them all.

Then she'd served penne pasta with crayfish in a sauce of cream with a touch of fresh chilli, followed by a delicate lemon sorbet to cleanse the palette.

For the main, she'd sourced some wild boar with Carlotta's help, and she'd casseroled it with fruit and lots of wine and garlic, reducing it to a rich, dark consistency. Massimo, yet again, had insisted on tasting it, dipping his finger in the sauce and sucking it, and said it was at least as good as Carlotta's great-nephew's. Carlotta agreed, and asked her for the recipe, which amazed her.

She'd served it on a chestnut, apple and sweet potato mash, with fresh green beans and fanned Chantenay carrots. And now it was time for the dessert, individual portions of perfectly set and delicate pannacotta under a spun sugar cage, with fresh autumn raspberries dusted with vanilla sugar and drizzled with dark chocolate. If that didn't impress them, nothing would, she thought with satisfaction.

She carried them through with Maria's help, set them down in front of all the guests and then left them to it. She put the coffee on to brew in Elisa's smaller kitchen, with homemade *petit fours* sitting ready on the side, and then headed back to her kitchen to start the massive clean-up operation.

But Massimo was in there, up to his wrists in suds, scrubbing pans. The dishwasher was sloshing quietly in the background, and there was no sign of Maria.

'I sent her home,' he said in answer to her question. 'It's getting late, and she's got a child.'

'I was going to pay her.'

'I've done it. Roberto's taken her home. Why don't you make us both a coffee while I finish this?'

She wasn't going to argue. Her head was aching, her feet were coming out in sympathy and she hadn't sat down for six hours. More, probably.

'Are they happy?'

She shrugged. 'They didn't say not and they seemed to eat it all, mostly.'

'Well, that's a miracle. There are some fussy women amongst them. I don't know why my mother bothers with them.'

He dried his hands and sat down opposite her, picking up his coffee. 'Well done,' he said, and the approval in his voice warmed her.

'I'll reserve judgement until I get your mother's verdict,' she said, because after all he hadn't been her client.

'Don't bother. It was the best food this house has seen in decades. You did an amazing job.'

'I loved it,' she confessed with a smile. 'It was great to do something a bit more challenging, playing with flavours and presentation and just having a bit of fun. I love it. I've always loved it.'

He nodded slowly. 'Yes, I can see that. And you're very good at it. I don't suppose there's any left?'

She laughed and went to the fridge. 'There's some of the boar casserole, and a spare panna-cotta. Haven't you eaten?'

He pulled a face. 'Kid's food,' he admitted. 'My father and I took them out for pizza. There didn't seem to be a lot of room in here.'

She plated him up some of the casserole with the vegetables, put it in the microwave and reheated it, then set it down in front of him and watched him eat. It was the best part of her job, to watch people enjoying the things she'd created, and he was savouring every mouthful.

She felt a wave of sadness and regret that there was no future for them, that she wouldn't spend the rest of her life creating wonderful, warming food and watching him eat it with relish.

She'd had the girls in with her earlier in the day, and she'd let them help her make the *petit fours* from homemade marzipan. That, too, had given her pangs of regret and a curious sense of loss. Silly, really. She'd never had them, so how could she feel that she'd lost them?

And after he'd eaten so much marzipan she was afraid he'd be sick, Antonino had stood up at the sink on an upturned box and washed up the plastic mixing bowls, soaking himself and the entire area in the process and having a great time with the bubbles. Such a sweet child, and the spitting image of his father. He was going to be a good-looking man one day, but she wouldn't be there to see it.

Or watch his father grow old.

She took away his plate, and replaced it with the pannacotta. He pressed the sugar cage with his fingertip, and frowned as it shattered gently onto the plate. 'How did you make it?' he asked, fascinated. 'I've never understood.'

'Boil sugar and water until it's caramelised, then trail it over an oiled mould. It's easy.'

He laughed. 'For you. I can't even boil an egg. Without Carlotta my kids would starve.'

'No. They'd eat pizza,' she said drily, and he gave a wry grin.

'Probably.' He dug the spoon into the panna-cotta and scooped up a raspberry with it, then sighed as it melted on his tongue. 'Amazing,' he mumbled, and scraped the plate clean.

Then he put the spoon down and pushed the plate away, leaning back and staring at her. 'You really are an exceptional chef. If there's any justice, you'll do well in your catering business. That was superb.'

'Thank you.' She felt his praise warm her, and somehow that was more important than anyone else's approval. She washed his plate and their coffee cups, then turned back to him, her mind moving on to the real reason she was here.

'Massimo, I need to talk to you about Jen and the wedding. They'll be here in two days, and I need to pick them up from the airport somehow.'

'I'll do it,' he offered instantly. 'My mother's preparing the guest wing for them, but she wanted to know if they needed one room or two.'

'Oh, one. Definitely. She needs help in the night sometimes. Is there a shower?'

'A wet room. That was one of the reasons for

the choice. And it's got French doors out to the terrace around the other side. Come. I'll show you. You can tell me which room would be the best for them.'

She went, and was blown away by their guest suite. Two bedrooms, both large, twin beds in one and a huge double in the other, with a wet room between and French doors out onto the terrace. And there was a small sitting room, as well, a private retreat, with a basic kitchen for making drinks and snacks.

'This will be just perfect. Give them the double room. She wakes in the night quite often, having flashbacks. They're worse if Andy's not beside her.'

'Poor girl.'

She nodded, still racked with guilt. She always would be, she imagined. It would never go away, just like his guilt over Angelina slumped over the kitchen table, unable to summon help.

She felt his finger under her chin, tilting her face up to his so he could look into her eyes.

'It was not your fault,' he said as if he could read her mind.

Her eyes were steady, but sad. 'Any more than

Angelina's death was your fault. Bad things happen. Guilt is just a natural human reaction. Knowing it and believing it are two different things.'

He felt his mouth tilt into a smile, but what kind of a smile it was he couldn't imagine. It faded, as he stared into her eyes, seeing the ache in them, the longing, the emptiness.

He needed her. Wanted her like he had never wanted anyone, but there was too much at stake to risk upsetting the status quo, for any of them.

He dropped his hand. 'What time do they arrive?' he asked, and the tension holding them eased.

For now.

They collected Jen and Andy from Pisa airport at midday on Friday, and they were blown away by their first view of the *palazzo*. By the time they'd pulled up at the bottom of the steps, Jen's eyes were like saucers, but all Lydia could think about was how her sister would get up the steps.

She hadn't even thought about it, stupidly, and now—

'Come here, gorgeous,' Andy said, unfazed by

the sight of them, and scooping Jen up, he grinned and carried her up the steps to where Roberto was waiting with the doors open.

Massimo and Lydia followed, carrying their luggage and the crutches, and as they reached the top their eyes met and held.

The memory was in her eyes, and it transfixed him. The last woman to be carried up those steps had been her in that awful wedding dress—the dress that was still hanging on the back of his office door, waiting for her to ask for it and burn it.

He should let her. Should burn it himself, instead of staring at it for hour after hour and thinking of her.

He dragged his eyes away and forced himself to concentrate on showing them to their rooms.

'I'll leave you with Lydia. If you need anything, I'll be in the office.'

And he walked away, crossing the courtyard with a firm, deliberate stride. She dragged her eyes off him and closed the door, her heart still pounding from that look they'd exchanged at the top of the steps.

Such a short time since he'd carried her up them, and yet so much had happened. Nothing obvious, nothing apparently momentous, and yet nothing would ever be quite the same as it had been before.

Starting with her sister's wedding.

'Wow—this is incredible!' Jen breathed, leaning back on Andy and staring out of the French doors at the glorious view. 'So beautiful! And the house—my God, Lydia, it's fantastic! Andy, did you see those paintings on the wall?'

Lydia gave a soft laugh. 'Those are the rough ones. There are some utterly stunning frescoes in the main part of the house, up the stairwell, for instance, and in the dining room. Absolutely beautiful. The whole place is just steeped in history.'

'And we're going to get married from here. I can't believe it.'

'Believe it.' She glanced at her watch. 'Are you hungry? There's some soup and cheese for lunch, and we'll eat properly tonight. Anita's coming over before dinner to talk to you and show you where the marquee will go and how it all works—they've had Carla's wedding and Luca's here, so they've done it all before.'

'Not Massimo's?'

She had no idea. It hadn't been mentioned. 'I

don't know. Maybe not. So—lunch. Do you want a lie down for a while, or shall I bring you something over?'

'Oh, I don't want to make work for you,' Jen said, but Lydia could see she was flagging, and she shook her head.

'I don't mind. I'll bring you both something and you can take it easy for a few hours. Travelling's always exhausting.'

Anita arrived at five, and by six Gio had put in an appearance, rather as she'd expected.

He found Lydia in the kitchen, and helped himself to a glass of Prosecco from the fridge and a handful of canapés.

'Hey,' she said, slapping his wrist lightly when he went back for more. 'I didn't know you were involved in the wedding planning.'

'I'm not,' he said with a cocky grin. 'I'm just here for the food.'

And Anita, she thought, but she didn't say that. She knew he'd turn from the smiling playboy to the razor-tongued lawyer the instant she mentioned the woman's name. Instead she did a little digging on another subject.

'So, how many weddings have there been here recently?' she asked.

'Two—Carla and Luca.'

'Not Massimo?'

'No. He got married in the *duomo* and they went back to her parents' house. Why?'

She shrugged. 'I just didn't want to say anything that hit a nerve.'

'I think you hit a nerve,' he said, 'even without speaking. You unsettle him.'

Was it so obvious? Maybe only to someone who was looking for trouble.

'Relax, Gio,' she said drily. 'You don't need to panic and get out your pre-nup template. This is going nowhere.'

'Shame,' he said, pulling a face, 'you might actually be good for him,' and while she was distracted he grabbed another handful of canapés.

She took the plate away and put it on the side. 'Shame?' she asked, and he shrugged.

'He's lonely. Luca likes you, so does Isabelle. And so does our mother, which can't be bad. She's a hard one to please.'

'Not as hard as her son,' she retorted. 'And talking of Massimo, why don't you go and find him and leave me in peace to cook? You're distracting me.'

'Wouldn't want to do that. You might ruin the food, and I've come all the way from Florence for it.'

And he sauntered off, stealing another mouthful from the plate in passing.

The dinner went well, and Anita came back the following day to go through the plans in detail, after talking to Jen and Andy the night before.

'She's amazing,' Jen said later. 'She just seems to know what I want, and she's got the answers to all of my questions.'

'Good,' she said, glad they'd got on well, because hearing the questions she'd realised there was no way someone without in-depth local knowledge could have answered them.

They were getting married the first weekend in May, in the town hall, and coming back to the *palazzo* for the marquee reception. They talked food, and she asked Anita for the catering budget and drew a blank. 'Whatever you need,' she was told, and she shook her head.

'I need to know.'

'I allow between thirty and eighty euros a head for food. Do whatever you want, he won't mind. Just don't make it cheap. That would insult him.'

'What about wine?'

'Prosecco for reception drinks, estate red and white for the meal, estate vinsanto for the dessert, champagne for toasts—unless you'd rather have prosecco again?'

'Prosecco would be fine. I prefer it,' Jen said, looking slightly stunned. 'Lydia, this seems really lavish.'

'Don't worry, Jen, she's earned it,' Anita said. 'He's been working her to the bone over the harvest season, and it's not finished yet.'

It wasn't, and there was a change in the weather. Saturday night was cold and clear, and there was a hint of frost on the railings. Winter was coming, and first thing on Monday morning Roberto, not Massimo, took Jen and Andy to the airport because *la Raccolta*, the olive harvest, was about to begin.

Jen hugged her goodbye, her eyes welling. 'It's going to be amazing. I don't know how to thank you.'

'You don't need to thank me. Just go home and

concentrate on getting better, and don't buy your wedding dress until I'm there. I don't want to miss that.'

'What, with your taste in wedding dresses?' Massimo said, coming up behind them with a teasing smile that threatened to double her blood pressure.

'It was five pounds!'

'You were cheated,' he said, laughing, and kissed Jen goodbye, slapping Andy on the back and wishing them a safe journey. 'I have to go—I'm needed at the plant. We have a problem with the olive press. I'll see you in May.'

She waved them off, feeling a pang of homesickness as they went, but she retreated to the kitchen where Carlotta was carving bread.

'Here we go again, then,' she said with a smile, and Carlotta smiled back and handed her the knife.

'I cut the *prosciutto*,' she said, and turned on the slicer.

He was late back that night—more problems with the *frantoio*, so Roberto told her, and Carlotta was exhausted.

Elisa and Vittorio were out for dinner, and so apart from Roberto and Carlotta, she was alone in the house with the children. And he was clearly worried for his wife.

'Go on, you go and look after her. Make her have an early night. I'll put the children to bed and look after them.'

'Are you sure?'

'Of course. They don't bite.'

He smiled gratefully and went, and she found the children in the sitting room. Antonino and Lavinia were squabbling again, and Francesca was on the point of tears.

'Who wants a story?' she asked, and they stopped fighting and looked up at her.

'Where's *Pàpa*?' Lavinia asked, looking doubtful.

'Working,' she said, because explaining what he was doing when she didn't really understand was beyond her. But they seemed to accept it, and apart from tugging his sister's hair again, even Antonino co-operated.

More or less. There was some argument about whether or not they needed a bath, but she was pretty sure no child had died from missing a single bath night, so she chivvied them into their pyjamas, supervised the teeth cleaning and ushered them into Antonino's bedroom.

It was a squeeze, but they all fitted on the bed somehow, and he handed her his favourite story book.

It was simple enough, just about, that she could fudge her way through it, but her pronunciation made them all laugh, and Francesca coached her. Then she read it again, much better this time, and gradually Antonino's eyelids began to wilt.

She sent the girls out, tucked him up and, on impulse, she kissed him goodnight.

He was already asleep by the time she reached the door, and Lavinia was in bed. Francesca, though, looked unhappy still, so after she'd settled her sister, she went into the older girl's room and gave her a hug.

She wasn't surprised when she burst into tears. She'd been on the brink of it before, and Lydia took her back downstairs and made her a hot drink and they curled up on the sofa in the sitting room next to the kitchen and talked.

'He's always working,' she said, her eyes welling again. 'He's never here, and Nino and Vinia always fight, and then Carlotta gets cross and upset because she's tired, and it's always me to stop them fighting, and—'

She broke off, her thin shoulders racked with sobs, and Lydia pulled her into her arms and rocked her, shushing her gently as she wept.

*'—she's the one who bears the brunt of the loss, because when I'm not there the little ones turn to her. She has to be mother to them, and she's been so strong, but she's just a little girl herself—'*

Poor, poor little thing. She was so stoic, trying to ease the burden on her beloved *pàpa*, and he was torn in half by his responsibilities. It was a no-win situation, and there was nothing she could do to change it, but maybe, just this one night, she'd made it a little easier.

She cradled Francesca in her arms until the storm of weeping had passed, and then they put on a DVD and snuggled up together to watch it.

Lydia couldn't understand it, but it didn't matter, and after a short while Francesca dropped off to sleep on Lydia's shoulder. She shifted her gently so she was lying with her head on her lap, and she stroked her hair as she settled again.

Dear, sweet child. Lydia was falling for her, she

realised. Falling for them all. For the first time in her life she felt truly at home, truly needed, as if what she did really made a difference.

She sifted the soft, dark curls through her fingers and wondered what the future held for her and for her brother and sister.

She'd never know. Her time here was limited, they all knew that, and yet she'd grown to love them all so much that to leave them, never to know what became of them, how their lives panned out—it seemed unthinkable. She felt so much a part of their family, and it would be so easy to imagine living here with them, maybe adding to the family in time.

She squeezed her eyes shut and bit her lips.

No. It was never going to happen. She was going, and she had to remember that.

But not yet, she thought, a fine tendril of hair curled around her finger. Not now. For now, she'd just sit there with Francesca, and they'd wait for Massimo to return.

It was so late.

His mother would have put the children to bed,

he thought, but yet again he'd missed their bedtime story, yet again he'd let them down.

The lights were on in the sitting room, and he could hear the television. Odd. He paused at the door, thinking the children must have left everything on, and he saw Lydia asleep on the sofa, Francesca sprawled across her lap.

Why Lydia? And why wasn't Francesca in bed?

He walked quietly over and looked down at them. They were both sound asleep, and Lydia was going to have a dreadful crick in her neck, but he was filthy, and if he was to carry Francesca up to bed, he needed a shower.

He backed out silently, went upstairs and showered, then threw on clean clothes and ran lightly downstairs.

'Lydia?' he murmured softly, touching her on the shoulder, and she stirred slightly and winced.

'Oh—you're home,' she whispered.

'*Si*. I'll take her.'

He eased her up into his arms, and Francesca snuggled close.

'She missed you,' Lydia said. 'The little ones were tired and naughty.'

'I'm sorry.'

'Don't be. It's not your fault.'

'Why are you here? My mother should be putting them to bed. I sent her a text.'

'They're out for dinner.'

He dropped his head back with a sigh. 'Of course. Oh, Lydia, I'm so sorry.'

'It's fine. Put her to bed.'

He did, settling her quickly, earning a sleepy smile as he kissed her goodnight. But by the time he got downstairs again, the television was off and the sitting room was in darkness.

It was over.

*La Raccolta* was finished, the olive oil safely in the huge lidded terracotta urns where it would mature for a while before being bottled.

The fresh olive oil, straight from the press, was the most amazing thing she'd ever tasted, and she'd used it liberally in the cooking and on *bruschetta* as an appetiser for the family's meals.

Of all the harvests, she'd found the olive harvest the most fascinating. The noise and smell in the pressing room was amazing, the huge stone wheels revolving on edge in the great stainless steel bowl of the *frantoio*, the olive press, crushing the olives to a purple paste. It was spread on circular felt discs and then stacked and pressed so that the oily juice dribbled out and ran into a vat, where it separated naturally, the bright green oil floating to the top.

Such a simple process, really, unchanged for centuries, and yet so very effective.

Everything in there had been covered in oil, the floor especially, and she knew that every time she smelt olive oil now, she'd see that room, hear the sound of the *frantoio* grinding the olives, see Massimo tossing olives in the palm of his hand, or checking the press, or laughing with one of the workers.

It would haunt her for the rest of her life, and the time had come so quickly.

She couldn't believe she was going, but she was. She'd grown to love it, not just because of him, but because of all his family, especially the children.

They were sad she was leaving, and on her last night she cooked them a special meal of their own, with a seafood risotto for their starter, and a pasta dish with chicken and pesto, followed by the dessert of frozen berries with hot white chocolate sauce that was always everyone's favourite.

'I don't want you to go,' Francesca said sadly as they finished clearing up.

Massimo, coming into the room as she said it, frowned. 'She has to go, *cara.* She has a business to run.'

'No, she doesn't. She has a job here, with us.'

Her heart squeezed. 'But I don't, sweetheart,' she said gently. 'I was only here to help Carlotta with the harvest. It's finished now. I can't just hang around and wait for next year. I have to go and cook for other people.'

'You could cook for us,' she reasoned, but Lydia shook her head.

'No. Carlotta would feel hurt. That's her job, to look after you. And your *pàpa* is right, I have to go back to my business.'

'Not go,' Lavinia said, her eyes welling. '*Pàpa, no*!' She ran to him, begging him in Italian, words she couldn't understand.

'What's she saying?' she asked, and Lavinia turned to look at her, tugging at her father and pleading, and he met her eyes reluctantly.

'She wants you to stay. She said—'

He broke off, but Francesca wouldn't let him stop.

'Tell her what Lavinia said, *Pàpa*,' she prompted, and he closed his eyes briefly and then went on.

'*Pàpa* is unhappy when aren't you're here,' he said grudgingly, translating directly as Lavinia spoke. 'Please don't go. We missed you when you went home before.' He hesitated, and she nudged him. 'It's lovely when you're here,' he went on, his bleak eyes locked with hers, 'because you make *Pàpa* laugh. He never laughs when you're not here.'

A tear slipped over and slid down her cheek, but she didn't seem to notice. Their eyes were locked, and he could see the anguish in them. He swallowed hard, his arm around Lavinia's skinny little shoulders holding her tight at his side.

Was it true? Was he unhappy when she wasn't there, unhappy enough that even the children could see it? Did he really not laugh when she wasn't there?

Maybe.

Lydia pressed her fingers to her lips, and shook her head. 'Oh, Lavinia. I'm sorry. I don't want to make your *pàpa* unhappy, or any of you, but I have to go home to my family.'

She felt little arms around her hips, and looked

down to find Antonino hugging her, his face buried in her side. She laid a hand gently on his hair and stroked it, aching unbearably inside. She'd done this, spent so much time with them that she was hurting them now by leaving, and she never meant to hurt them. 'I'm sorry,' she said to him, *'mi dispiace.'* And his little arms tightened.

'Will you read us a story?' Francesca asked.

She'd be leaving for the airport before three in the morning, long before the children were up, so this was her last chance to read to them. Her last chance ever? 'Of course I will,' she said, feeling choked. She'd done it a few times since the night of the *frantoio* breakdown, and she loved it. Too much.

They were already in their pyjamas, and she ushered them up to bed, supervised the teeth cleaning as she'd done before, and then they settled down on Antonino's bed, all crowded round while she read haltingly to them in her awful, amateurish Italian.

She could get the expressions right, make it exciting—that was the easy bit. The pronunciation was harder, but it was a book they knew, so it didn't really matter.

What mattered was lying propped up against the wall, with Antonino under one arm and Lavinia under the other, and Francesca curled up by her knees leaning against the wall and watching her with wounded eyes.

She was the only one of them to remember her mother, and for a few short weeks, Lydia realised, she'd slipped into the role without thinking, unconsciously taking over some of the many little things a mother did. Things like making cupcakes, and birthday cards for Roberto. She'd stopped the two little ones fighting, and hugged them when they'd hurt themselves, and all the time she'd been playing happy families and ignoring the fact that she'd be going away soon, going back to her real life at home.

And now she had to go.

She closed the book, and the children snuggled closer, stretching out the moment.

Then Massimo's frame filled the doorway, his eyes shadowed in the dim light.

'Come on. Bedtime now. Lydia needs to pack.'

It was a tearful goodnight, for all of them, and as soon as she could she fled to her room, stifling the tears.

She didn't have to pack. She'd done it ages ago, been round all the places she might have left anything, and there was nothing to do now, nothing to distract her.

Only Lavinia's words echoing in her head.

*He never laughs when you're not here.*

The knock was so quiet she almost didn't hear it.

'Lydia?'

She opened the door, unable to speak, and met his tortured eyes.

And then his arms closed around her, and he held her hard against his chest while she felt the shudders run through him.

They stayed like that for an age, and then he eased back and looked down at her.

His eyes were raw with need, and she led him into the room and closed the door.

Just one last time…

# CHAPTER TEN

'IS IT true?'

He turned his head and met her eyes in the soft glow of the bedside light, and his face was shuttered and remote.

'Is what true?'

'That you don't laugh when I'm not here?'

He looked away again. 'You don't want to listen to what the children say.'

'Why not, if it's true? Is it?'

He didn't answer, so she took it as a yes. It made her heart ache. If only he'd believe in them, if only he'd let her into his heart, his life, but all he would say was no.

'Talk to me,' she pleaded.

He turned his head back, his eyes unreadable.

'What is there to say?'

'You could tell me how you really feel. That would be a good start.'

He laughed, a harsh, abrupt grunt full of pain. 'I can't,' he said, his accent stronger than she'd ever heard it. 'I can't find the words, I don't have the language to do this in English.'

'Then tell me in Italian. I won't understand, but you can say it then out loud. You can tell me whatever you like, and I can't hold you to it.'

He frowned, but then he reached out and stroked her face, his fingers trembling. His mouth flickered in a sad smile, and then he started to speak, as if she'd released something inside him that had been held back for a long, long time.

She didn't understand it, but she understood the tone—the gentleness, the anguish, the pain of separation.

And then, his eyes locked with hers, he said softly, *'Ciao, mia bella ragazza. Te amo...'*

She reached out and cradled his jaw, her heart breaking. *Ciao* meant hello, but it also meant goodbye.

'It doesn't have to be goodbye,' she said softly. 'I love you, too—so much.'

He shook his head. 'No. No, *cara*, please. I can't let you love me. I can't let you stay. You'll be hurt.'

'No!'

'Yes. I won't let you.'

'Would you stop that?' she demanded, angry now. 'The first time I met you, you said I couldn't go in the plane with Nico because it wasn't safe. Now you're telling me I can't love you because I'll get hurt! Maybe I want to take the risk, Massimo? Maybe I *need* to take the risk.'

'No. You have a life waiting for you, and one day there will be some lucky man…'

'I don't want another man, I want you.'

'No! I have nothing to give you. I'm already pulled in so many ways. How can I be fair to you, or the children, or my work, my family? How can I do another relationship justice?'

'Maybe I could help you. Maybe I could make it easier. Maybe we could work together?'

'No. You love your family, you have your career. If I let you give it all up for me, what then? What happens when we've all let you into our hearts and then you leave?'

'I won't leave!'

'You don't know that. You've been here less than three months. What happens in three years, when we have another child and you decide you're unhappy and want to go? I don't have time for you,

I can't give you what you need. I don't even have enough time now to sleep! Please, *cara*. Don't make it harder. You'll forget me soon.'

'No. I'll never forget you. I'll never stop loving you.'

'You will. You'll move on. You'll meet someone and marry him and have children of your own in England, close to your family, and you'll look back and wonder what you saw in this sad and lonely old man.'

'Don't be ridiculous, you're not old, and you're only sad and lonely because you won't let anybody in!'

His eyes closed, as if he couldn't bear to look at her any longer. 'I can't. The last time I let anyone into my life, she lost her own, and it was because I was too busy, too tired, too overstretched to be there for her.'

'It wasn't your fault!'

'Yes, it was! I was *here*! I was supposed to be looking after her, but I was lying in my bed asleep while she was dying.'

'She should have woken you! She should have told you she was sick. It was not your fault!'

'No? Then why do I wake every night hearing her calling me?'

He threw off the covers and sat up, his legs over the edge of the bed, his head in his hands, his whole body vibrating with tension. 'I can't do this, Lydia! Please, don't ask me to. I can't do it.'

*Why do I wake every night hearing her calling me?*

His words echoing in her head, her heart pounding, she knelt up behind him, her arms around him, her body pressed to his in comfort.

'It wasn't your fault,' she said gently. 'You weren't responsible, but you're holding yourself responsible, and you have to forgive yourself. It wasn't my fault Jen had her accident, but I've blamed myself, and it has taken months to accept that it wasn't my fault and to forgive myself for not stopping him. You have to do the same. You have to accept that you weren't at fault—'

'But I was! I should have checked on her.'

'You were asleep! What time of year was it?'

'Harvest,' he admitted, his voice raw. 'The end of *La Raccolta*.'

Right at the end of the season. Now, in fact. Any

time now. Her heart contracted, and she sank back down onto her feet, her hands against his back.

'You were exhausted, weren't you? Just as you're exhausted now. And she didn't want to disturb you, so she went down to the kitchen for painkillers.'

He sucked in a breath, and she knew she was right.

'She probably wasn't thinking clearly. Did she suffer from headaches?'

'Yes. All the time. They said she had a weakness in the vessels.'

'So it could have happened at any time?'

'*Si*. But it happened when I was there, and it happened slowly, and if I'd realised, if I hadn't thought she was with the baby, if I'd known…'

'If you'd been God, in fact? If you'd been able to see inside her head?'

'They could have seen inside her head. She'd talked of going to the doctor about her headaches, but we were too busy, and she'd just had the baby, and it was the harvest, and…'

'And there was just no time. Oh, Massimo. I'm so sorry, but you know it wasn't your fault. You can't blame yourself.'

'Yes, I can. I can, and I have to, because my guilt and my grief is all I have left to give her! I can't even love her any more because you've taken that from me!' he said harshly, his voice cracking.

The pain ran through her like a shockwave.

How could he tell her that he loved her, and yet cling to his guilt and grief so that he could hold onto Angelina?

He couldn't. Not if he really loved her. Unless…

'Why are you doing this to me?' she asked quietly. 'To yourself? To your children? You wear your grief and your guilt like a hair shirt to torture yourself with, but it's not just you you're torturing, you're torturing me, as well, and your children. And they don't deserve to be tortured just because you're too much of a coward to let yourself love again!'

'I am not a coward!'

'Then prove it!' she begged. 'Let yourself love again!'

He didn't answer, his shoulders rigid, unmoving, and after what felt like forever, she gave up. She'd tried, and she could do no more.

Shaking, she eased away from him and glanced at her watch.

'We have to leave in half an hour. I'm going to shower,' she said, as steadily as she could.

And she walked into the bathroom, closed the door and let the tears fall…

He didn't come into the airport building this time.

He gave her a handful of notes to pay for her excess baggage, put her luggage on the pavement at the drop-off point and then hesitated.

'I'll see you in May,' he said, his voice clipped and harsh.

His eyes were raw with pain, and she wanted to weep for him, and for herself, and for the children, but now wasn't the time.

'Yes. I'll be in touch.'

'Anita will email you. She's in charge. I'll be too busy.'

Of course he would.

'Take care of yourself,' she said softly. And going up on tiptoe, she pressed her lips to his cheek.

His arms came round her, and for the briefest moment he rested his head against hers. *'Ciao, bella,'* he said softly, so softly that she scarcely heard him, and then he was straightening up, moving back, getting into the car.

He started the engine and drove away, and she watched his tail lights until they disappeared. Then she gathered up her luggage and headed for the doors.

It was the worst winter of her life.

The weather was glorious, bright winter sunshine that seemed to bounce right off her, leaving her cold inside. She found work in the pub down the road, and she created a website and tried to promote her catering business.

It did well, better than she'd expected, but without him her life was meaningless.

Jen found her one day in mid-January, staring into space.

'Hey,' she said softly, and came and perched beside her on the back of the sofa, staring out across the valley.

'Hey yourself. How are you doing?'

'OK. We've had another email from Anita. She wants to know about food.'

She could hardly bring herself to think about food. For a while she'd thought she was pregnant she'd felt so sick, but she wasn't. The test said no, her body said no and her heart grieved for a child that never was and never would be. And still she felt sick.

'What does she want to know? I've given her menu plans.'

'Something about the carpaccio of beef?'

She sighed. 'OK. I'll contact her.'

It was nothing to do with the beef. It was about Massimo.

'He's looking awful,' Anita said. 'He hasn't smiled since you left.'

*Nor have I,* she thought, *but there's nothing I can do, either for him or me.*

She didn't reply to the email. Two hours later her phone rang.

'I can't help you, Anita,' she said desperately. 'He won't listen to me.'

'He won't listen to anyone—Luca, Carlotta, his mother—even Gio's on your side, amazingly, but he just says he doesn't want to talk about it. And we're all worried. We're really worried.'

'I'm sorry, I can't do any more,' she said again, choked, and hung up.

Jen found her in her room, face down on the bed

sobbing her heart out, and she lay down beside her and held her, and gradually it stopped hurting and she was numb again.

Better, in a strange kind of way.

January turned into February, and then March, and finally Jen was able to walk without the crutches.

'That's amazing,' Lydia said, hugging her, her eyes filling with tears. 'I'm so glad.'

'So am I.' Jen touched her cheek gently. 'I'm all right now, Lydia. I'm going to be OK. Please stop hurting yourself about it.'

'I'm not,' she said, and realised it was true, to an extent. Oh, it would always hurt to know that she'd been part of the sequence of events that had led to Jen's accident, but she'd stopped taking the blame for it, and now she could share in the joy of Jen's recovery. If only Massimo…

'You need to buy your wedding dress, we're leaving it awfully late,' she said, changing the subject before her mind dragged her off down that route.

'I know. There's a shop in town that does them to take away, so they don't need to be ordered. Will you come with me?'

She ignored the stab of pain, and hugged her sister. 'Of course I will.'

It was bittersweet.

They all went together—Lydia, Jen and their mother and she found a dress that laced up the back, with an inner elasticated corset that was perfect for giving her some extra back support.

'Oh, that's so comfy!' she said, and then looked in the mirror and her eyes filled.

'Oh…'

Lydia grabbed her mother's hand and hung on. It was definitely The Dress, and everybody's eyes were filling now.

'Oh, darling,' her mother said, and hugged her, laughing and crying at the same time, because it might never have come to this. They could have lost her, and yet here she was, standing on her own two feet, unaided, and in her wedding dress. Their tears were well and truly earned.

After she'd done another twirl and taken the dress off, the manageress of the little wedding shop poured them another glass of Prosecco to toast Jen's choice.

As the bubbles burst in her mouth, Lydia closed her eyes and thought of him.

Sitting on the terrace outside her bedroom, sipping Prosecco and talking into the night. They'd done it more than once, before the weather had turned. Pre-dinner drinks when Jen and Andy had come to visit. Sitting in the *trattoria* waiting for their food to come, the second time they'd made love.

'Lydia?'

She opened her eyes and dredged up a smile. 'You looked stunning in it, Jen. Absolutely beautiful. Andy'll be bowled over.'

'What about you?'

'I don't need a wedding dress!' she said abruptly, and then remembered she was supposed to be Jen's bridesmaid, and suddenly it was all too much.

'Can we do this another day?' she asked desperately, and Jen, seeing something in her eyes, nodded.

'Of course we can.'

She went back on her own a few days later, and flicked through the rails while she was waiting.

And there, on a mannequin in the corner, was the most beautiful dress she'd ever seen.

The softest, heaviest silk crepe de Chine, cut on the cross and hanging beautifully, it was exquisite. So soft, she thought, fingering it with longing, such a far cry from the awful thing she'd worn for the competition, and she wondered, stupidly, if she'd worn it instead, would she have fallen? And if not, would she have known what it was to love him? Maybe, if he'd seen her wearing a dress like that…

'It's a beautiful dress, isn't it? Why don't you try it on?'

'I don't need a wedding dress,' she said bluntly, dropping her hand to her side. 'I'm here for a bridesmaid's dress.'

'You could still try it on. We're quiet today, and I'd love to see it on you. You've got just the figure for it.'

How on earth had she let herself be talked into it? Because, of course, it fitted like a dream on her hourglass figure, smoothing her hips, showing off her waist, emphasising her bust.

For a moment—just a moment—she let herself

imagine his face as he saw her in it. She'd seen that look before, when he'd been making love to her—

'This is silly,' she said, desperate to take it off now. 'I'm not getting married.'

Not ever…

The awful wedding dress was still hanging on the back of his door.

He stared at it numbly. It still had her blood on it, a dark brown stain on the bodice where she'd wiped her fingers after she'd touched the graze on her head.

He missed her. The ache never left him, overlying the other ache, the ache that had been there since Angelina died.

Their wedding photo was still on his desk, and he picked it up and studied it. Was Lydia right? Was her wearing a metaphorical hair shirt, punishing himself for what was really not his fault?

Rationally, he knew that, but he couldn't let it go.

Because he hadn't forgiven himself? Or because he was a coward?

*It's not just you you're torturing, you're tor-*

*turing me, as well, and your children. And they don't deserve to be tortured just because you're too much of a coward to let yourself love again!*

Getting up from the desk, he went and found Carlotta and told her he was going out. And then he did what he should have done a long time ago.

He went to the place where she was buried, and he said goodbye, and then he went home and took off his wedding ring. There was an inscription inside. It read *'Amor vincit omnia'.*

Love conquers everything.

Could it? Not unless you gave it a chance, he thought, and pressing the ring to his lips, he nestled it in Angelina's jewellery box, with the lock of her hair, the first letter she'd ever sent him, a rose from her bouquet.

And then he put the box away, and went outside into the garden and stood at the railings, looking out over the valley below. She'll be here soon, he thought, and then I'll know.

Jen and Andy saw her off at the airport.

She put on a bright face, but in truth she was dreading this part of the wedding.

She was going over early to finalise the menu

and meet the people who were going to be helping her. Carlotta's nephew, the owner of the *trattoria*, had loaned her one of his chefs and sourced the ingredients, and the waiting staff were all from local families and had worked for Anita before, but the final responsibility for the menu and the food was hers.

None of that bothered her. She was confident about the menu, confident in the ability of the chef and the waiting staff, and the food she was sure would be fine.

It was seeing Massimo that filled her with dread.

Dread, and longing.

She was thinner.

Thinner, and her face was drawn. She looked as if she'd been working too hard, and he wondered how her business was going. Maybe she'd been too successful?

He hoped not—no! That was wrong. If it was going well, if it was what she wanted, then he must let her go.

Pain stabbed through him and he sucked in a breath. For the past few weeks he'd put thoughts of failure out of his mind, but now—now, seeing her there, they all came rushing to the fore.

He walked towards her, and as if she sensed him there she turned her head and met his eyes. All the breath seemed to be sucked out of his body, and he had to tell his feet how to move.

*'Ciao, bella,'* he said softly, and her face seemed to crumple slightly.

*'Ciao,'* she said, her voice uneven, and then he hugged her, because she looked as if she'd fall down if he didn't.

'Is this everything?'

She nodded, and he took the case from her and wheeled it out of the airport to his car.

He was looking well, she thought. A little thinner, perhaps, but not as bad as she'd thought from what Anita had said. Because he was over her?

She felt a sharp stab of pain, and sucked in her breath. Maybe he'd been right. Maybe he couldn't handle it, and he'd just needed to get back onto an even keel again.

And then he came round and opened the car door for her, and she noticed his wedding ring was missing, and her heart began to thump.

Was it significant?

She didn't know, and he said nothing, just smiled at her as he got into the car and talked about what the children had been up to and how the wedding preparations were going, all the way back to the *palazzo.*

It was like coming home, she thought.

The children were thrilled to see her, especially Francesca who wrapped her arms around her and hugged her so hard she thought her ribs might break.

'Goodness, you've all grown so tall!' she said, her eyes filling. Lavinia's arms were round her waist, and Antonino was hanging on her arm and jumping up and down. It made getting up the steps a bit of a challenge, but they managed it, and Massimo just chuckled softly and carried her luggage in.

'I've put you in the same room,' he said, and she felt a shiver of dread. The last time she'd been in here, he'd broken her heart. She wasn't sure she wanted to be there again, but it felt like her room now, and it would be odd to be anywhere else.

'So, what's the plan?' she asked as he put her case down.

He smiled wryly. 'Anita's coming over. I've told her to give you time to unwind, but she said there was too much to do. Do you want a cup of tea?'

'I'd love a cup of tea,' she said fervently. 'But don't worry. I'll make it.'

He nodded. 'In that case, I'll go and get on. You know my mobile number—ring me if you need me.'

She didn't have time to need him, which was perhaps just as well. The next few days were a whirlwind, and by the time the family arrived, she was exhausted.

Anita was brilliant. She organised everything, made sure everyone knew what they were to do and kept them all calm and focused, and the day of the wedding went without a hitch.

Lydia's involvement in the food was over. She'd prepared the starters and the deserts, the cold buffet was in the refrigerated van beside the marquee, and all she had to do was dress her sister and hold her bouquet.

And catch it, apparently, when it was all over.

Jen wasn't subtle. She stood just a few feet from

her, with everyone standing round cheering, and threw it straight at Lydia.

It hit her in the chest and she nearly dropped it, but then she looked up and caught Massimo's eye, and her heart began to pound slowly.

He was smiling.

Smiling? Why? Because he was glad it was all over? Or because the significance of her catching it wasn't lost on him?

She didn't know. She was too tired to care, and after Andy scooped his glowing, blushing bride up in his arms and carried her off at the end of the reception in a shower of confetti and good wishes, she took the chance and slipped quietly away.

There was so much to do—a mountain of clearing up in the kitchen in the *palazzo*, never mind all the catering equipment which had been hired in and had to be cleaned and returned.

Plates, cutlery, glasses, table linen.

'I thought I might find you in here.'

She looked up.

'There's a lot to do.'

'I know.'

He wasn't smiling. Not now. He was thoughtful. Maybe a little tense?

He took off his suit jacket and rolled up his sleeves and pitched in alongside her, and for a while they worked in silence. He changed the washing up water three times, she used a handful of tea towels, but finally the table was groaning with clean utensils.

'Better. The guests are leaving. Do you want to say goodbye?'

She smiled slightly and shook her head. 'They're not my guests. Let my parents do it. I've got enough to do.'

'I'll go and clear up outside,' he said, and she nodded. There was still a lot to do in there, and she worked until she was ready to drop.

Her feet hurt, her shoes were long gone and she wanted to lie down. The rest, she decided, would keep, and turning off the light, she headed back to her room.

She passed her parents in the colonnaded walkway around the courtyard, on their way in with Massimo's parents.

They stopped to praise the food yet again, and Elisa hugged her. 'It was wonderful. I knew it would be. You have an amazing talent.'

'I know,' her mother said. 'We're very proud of her.'

She was hugged and kissed again, and then she excused herself and finally got to her room, pausing in surprise in the doorway.

The door was open, the bedside light was on, and the bed was sprinkled with rose petals.

Rose petals?

She picked one up, lifting it to her nose and smelling the delicately heady fragrance.

Who—?

'May I come in?'

She spun round, the rose petal falling from her fingers, and he was standing there with a bottle of sparkling water and two glasses. 'I thought you might be thirsty,' he said.

'I don't know what I am,' she said. 'Too tired to know.'

He laughed softly, and she wondered—just briefly, with the small part of her brain that was still functioning—how often he'd done that since she went away.

'Lie down before you fall.'

She didn't need telling twice. She didn't bother to take the dress off. It was probably ruined anyway, and realistically when would she wear it again? She didn't go to dressy events very often. She flopped onto the bed, and he went round the other side, kicked off his shoes and settled himself beside her, propped up against the headboard.

'Here, drink this,' he said, handing her a glass, and she drained the water and handed the glass back.

'More.'

He laughed—again?—and refilled it, then leant back and sighed.

'Good wedding.'

'It was. Thank you. Without you, it wouldn't have happened.'

'It might have been at the hotel.'

'No. Nobody was giving me a lift—well, only Nico, and we both know how that might have ended.'

'Don't.' He took the empty glass from her again, put them both down and slid down the bed so he was lying flat beside her. His hand reached out, and their fingers linked and held.

'How are you, really?' he asked softly.

He wasn't talking about tonight, she realised,

and decided she might as well be honest. It was the only thing she had left.

'All right, I suppose. I've missed you.'

'I've missed you, too. I didn't know I could hurt as much as that, not any more. Apparently I can.'

She rolled to her side to face him, and he did the same, his smile gone now, his eyes serious.

'Massimo,' she said, cutting to the chase, 'where's your wedding ring?'

'Ah, *cara*. So observant. I took it off. I didn't need it any more. You were right, it was time to let the past go and move on with my life.'

'Without guilt?'

His smile was sad. 'Without guilt. With regret, perhaps. The knowledge that things probably wouldn't have been very different whatever I'd done. I'd lost sight of that. And you?' he added. 'Are you moving on with your life?'

She tried to laugh, but she was too tired and too hurt to make it believable. 'No. My business is going well, but I don't care. It's all meaningless without you.'

'Oh, *bella*,' he said softly, and reached for her. 'My life is the same. The only thing that's kept me going the last few weeks has been the knowledge that I'd see you again soon. Without that I would have gone insane. I nearly did go insane.'

'I know. Anita rang me. They were all worried about you.'

He eased her up against his chest, so that her face lay against the fine silk shirt, warm from his skin, the beat of his heart echoing in her ear, slow and steady.

'Stay with me,' he said. 'I have no right to ask you, after I sent you away like that, but I can't live without you. No. That's not true. I can. I just don't want to, because without you, I don't laugh. Lavinia was right. I don't laugh because there's nothing to laugh at when you're not here. Nothing seems funny, everything is cold and colourless and futile. The days are busy but monotonous, and the nights—the nights are so lonely.'

She swallowed a sob, and lifted her hand and cradled his stubbled jaw. 'I know. I've lain awake night after night and missed you. I can fill the days, but the nights…'

'The nights are endless. Cold and lonely and endless. I've tried working, but there comes a time when I have to sleep, and then every time I close my eyes, I see you.'

'Not Angelina?'

'No. Not Angelina. I said goodbye to her. I hadn't done it. I hadn't grieved for her properly, I'd buried myself in work and I thought I was all right, but then I met you and I couldn't love you as you deserved because I wasn't free. And instead of freeing myself, I sent you away.'

'I'm sorry. It must have been hard.'

His eyes softened, and he smiled and shook his head. 'No. It was surprisingly easy. I was ready to do it—more than ready. And I'm ready to move on. I just need to know that you're ready to come with me.'

She smiled and bit her lip. 'Where are we going?'

'Wherever life takes us. It will be here, because this is who I am and where I have to be, but what we do with that life is down to us.'

He took her hand from his cheek and held it, staring intently into her eyes. 'Marry me, Lydia. You've set me free, but that freedom is no use to me without you. I love you, *bella. Te amo.* If you still love me, if you haven't come to your senses in all this time, then marry me. Please.'

'Of course I'll marry you,' she breathed, her heart overflowing. 'Oh, you foolish, silly, wonderful man, of course I'll marry you! Just try and stop me. And I'll never, never stop loving you.'

'I've still got the dress,' he told her some time later, his eyes sparkling with mischief. 'It's hanging on my office door. I thought I'd keep it, just in case you said yes.'

Did the woman in the wedding dress shop have second sight? 'I think I might treat myself to a new one,' she said, and smiled at him.

They were married in June, in the town hall where Jen and Andy had been married.

It had been a rush—she'd had to pack up all her things in England and ship them over, and they'd moved, on his parents' insistence, into the main part of the *palazzo*.

A new start, a clean slate.

It would take some getting used to, but as Massimo said, it was a family home and it should have children in it. It was where he and his brothers and sisters had been brought up, and it was family tradition for the eldest son to take over the formal rooms of the *palazzo*. And hopefully, there would be other children to fill it.

She held onto that thought. She'd liked the simplicity of the other wing, but there was much more elbow room in the central part, essential if they were to have more children, and the views were, if anything, even more stunning. And maybe one day she'd grow into the grandeur.

But until their wedding night, she was still using the room she'd always had, and it was in there that Jen and her mother helped her put on the beautiful silk dress. It seemed woefully extravagant for such a small and simple occasion, but she was wearing it for him, only for him, and when she walked out to meet him, her heart was in her mouth.

He was waiting for her in the frescoed courtyard, and his eyes stroked slowly over her. He said nothing, and for an endless moment she thought he hated it. But then he lifted his eyes to hers, and the heat in them threatened to set her on fire.

She looked stunning.

He'd thought she was beautiful in the other wedding dress, much as he'd hated it. In this, she was spectacular. It hugged her curves like a lover, and just to look at her made him ache.

She wasn't wearing a veil, and the natural curls of her fine blonde hair fell softly to her shoulders. It was the way he liked it. Everything about her was the way he liked it, and at last he found a smile.

*'Mia bella ragazza,'* he said softly, and held out his hand to her.

It was a beautiful, simple ceremony.

Their vows, said by both of them in both English and Italian, were from the heart, and they were witnessed by their closest family and friends. Both sets of parents, his three sisters, Jen and Andy, Luca and Isabelle, Gio, Anita, Carlotta and Roberto, and of course the children.

Francesca and Lavinia were bridesmaids, and Antonino was the ring bearer. There was a tense moment when he wobbled and the rings started to slide, but it was all right, and with a smile of encouragement for his son, Massimo took her ring from the little cushion and slid it onto her finger, his eyes locked with hers.

He loved her. When he'd lost Angelina, he'd thought he could never love again, but Lydia had shown him the way. There was always room for love, he realised, always room for another person in your heart, and his heart had made room for her. How had he ever thought it could do otherwise?

She slid the other ring onto his finger, her fingers firm and confident, and he cupped her shoulders in his hands and bent his head and kissed her.

*'Te amo,'* he murmured, and then his words were drowned out by the clapping and cheering of their family.

Afterwards they went for lunch to the little *trattoria* owned by Carlotta's nephew. He did them proud. They drank Prosecco and ate simple, hearty food exquisitely cooked, and when it was over, they drove back to the *palazzo*. The others were going back to Luca and Isabelle's for the rest of the day, to give them a little privacy, and Massimo intended to take full advantage of it.

He drove up to the front door, scooped her up in his arms and carried her up the steps. The last time he'd done this she'd been bloodstained and battered. This time—this time she was his wife, and he felt like the luckiest man alive.

Pausing at the top he turned, staring out over the valley spread out below them. Home, he thought, his heart filled with joy, and Lydia rested her head on his shoulder and sighed.

'It's so beautiful.'

'Not as beautiful as you. And that dress…' He nuzzled her neck, making her arch against him. 'I've been wanting to take it off you all day.'

'Don't you like it? I wasn't sure myself. I thought maybe I should have stuck to the other one,' she teased, and he laughed, the sound carrying softly on the night air.

It was a sound she'd never tire of, she thought contentedly as he turned, still smiling, and carried his bride over the threshold.

* * * * *

**A VOW OF OBLIGATION**
Lynne Graham

**DEFYING DRAKON**
Carole Mortimer

**PLAYING THE GREEK'S GAME**
Sharon Kendrick

**ONE NIGHT IN PARADISE**
Maisey Yates

**VALTIERI'S BRIDE**
Caroline Anderson

**THE NANNY WHO KISSED HER BOSS**
Barbara McMahon

**FALLING FOR MR MYSTERIOUS**
Barbara Hannay

**THE LAST WOMAN HE'D EVER DATE**
Liz Fielding

**HIS MAJESTY'S MISTAKE**
Jane Porter

**DUTY AND THE BEAST**
Trish Morey

**THE DARKEST OF SECRETS**
Kate Hewitt

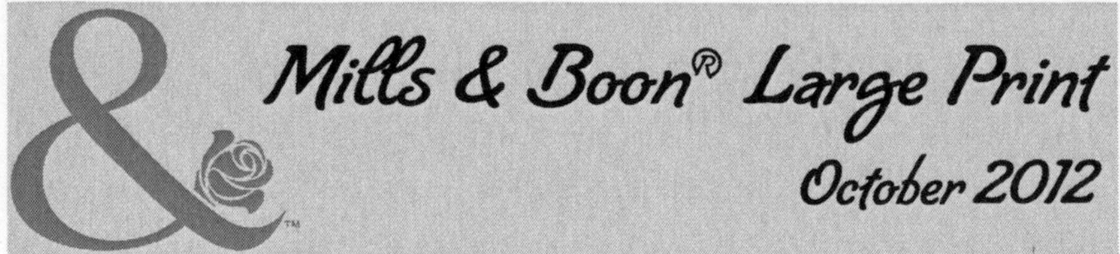


**A SECRET DISGRACE**
Penny Jordan

**THE DARK SIDE OF DESIRE**
Julia James

**THE FORBIDDEN FERRARA**
Sarah Morgan

**THE TRUTH BEHIND HIS TOUCH**
Cathy Williams

**PLAIN JANE IN THE SPOTLIGHT**
Lucy Gordon

**BATTLE FOR THE SOLDIER'S HEART**
Cara Colter

**THE NAVY SEAL'S BRIDE**
Soraya Lane

**MY GREEK ISLAND FLING**
Nina Harrington

**ENEMIES AT THE ALTAR**
Melanie Milburne

**IN THE ITALIAN'S SIGHTS**
Helen Brooks

**IN DEFIANCE OF DUTY**
Caitlin Crews